Dulc
Body For Ten Long Months

to have it thrown in her face first thing in the morning was simply too much.

He was oblivious to her presence in the doorway. He was talking to her baby, and she didn't miss the rapt look on Ryan's face at the sound of his father's voice.

Deep inside her, a feeling of helplessness rose. Ryan had been hers alone for almost a year. Now everything was going to have to change....

Tye wanted—no, *expected*—her to marry him. He had to be crazy! They barely knew each other.

But a vivid image of just how well they did know each other arose in her mind....

Dear Reader,

This month, we begin HOLIDAY HONEYMOONS, a wonderful new cross-line continuity series written by two of your favorites—Merline Lovelace and Carole Buck. The series begins in October with Merline's *Halloween Honeymoon*. Then, once a month right through February, look for holiday love stories by Merline and Carole—in Desire for November, Intimate Moments for December, back to Desire in January and concluding in Intimate Moments for Valentine's Day. Sound confusing? It's not—we'll keep you posted as the series continues…and I personally guarantee that these books are keepers!

And there are other goodies in store for you. Don't miss the fun as Cathie Linz's delightful series THREE WEDDINGS AND A GIFT continues with *Seducing Hunter*. And Lass Small's MAN OF THE MONTH, *The Texas Blue Norther*, is simply scrumptious.

Those of you who want an *ultrasensuous* love story need look no further than *The Sex Test* by Patty Salier. She's part of our WOMEN TO WATCH program highlighting brand-new writers. Warning: this book is HOT!

Readers who can't get enough of cowboys shouldn't miss Anne Marie Winston's *Rancher's Baby*. And if you're partial to a classic amnesia story (as I certainly am!), be sure to read Barbara McCauley's delectable *Midnight Bride*.

And, as always, I'm here to listen to you—so don't be afraid to write and tell me your thoughts about Desire!

Until next month,

Lucia Macro

Senior Editor

Please address questions and book requests to:
Silhouette Reader Service
U.S.: 3010 Walden Ave., P.O. Box 1325, Buffalo, NY 14269
Canadian: P.O. Box 609, Fort Erie, Ont. L2A 5X3

ANNE MARIE WINSTON

RANCHER'S BABY

SILHOUETTE *Desire*

Published by Silhouette Books

America's Publisher of Contemporary Romance

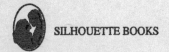

SILHOUETTE BOOKS

ISBN 0-373-76031-0

RANCHER'S BABY

Copyright © 1996 by Anne Marie Rodgers

ANNE MARIE WINSTON

A native Pennsylvanian and former educator, Anne Marie is a book lover, an animal lover and always a teacher at heart. She and her husband have two daughters and a menagerie of four-footed family members. When she's not parenting, writing or reading, she devotes her time to a variety of educational efforts in her community. Readers can write to Anne Marie at P.O. Box 302, Zullinger, PA 17272.

For Elise—
With XOXO & lotsa love to my small
but mighty Lisabettybelle

One

Tye Bradshaw squinted into the sun as the driver turned the four-wheel-drive pick-up truck off the highway. His head felt as if someone were playing a very large kettle drum just behind his eyes, and his broken finger throbbed.

The rancher who had offered to drop him off at the ranch maneuvered the truck between two stone pillars. They supported a black iron arch with a sign that proclaimed, Red Arrow Ranch, though for the life of him, Tye couldn't see anything that looked vaguely like a house or a barn. As the truck followed an unpaved road that bisected a large, flat plain of scrub and dusty earth, all Tye could see were cattle in the distance, their outlines wavering in the heat of the day.

So this was the Kincaid spread. This was where he would find Dulcie.

Ever since the single night they'd shared, he'd been unable to forget her. His mood darkened as he recalled the way she'd skedaddled out of his apartment in the morning, mortified at herself and too embarrassed to look him in the eye. He'd intended to go after her, but then the phone rang... and here he was, almost a year later, hoping she would accept a belated apology.

His thoughts were shaken right out of his head when the truck lumbered over a particularly big rut and bounced up, down and up again with an agonizing jolt. He gritted his teeth against the pain and let the rancher's off-key humming fill the silence until finally they crested a small rise. The Kincaid ranch buildings were spread out before them.

Despite his pain and discomfort, anticipation rose within him. Dulcie was here, probably in the big house that sat off to one side of the barns and corrals. The Good Samaritan drove right up to the yard that fronted the house. A black-and-white dog that looked like a cross between a border collie and a shepherd exploded from under the front porch, barking furiously just as the front door opened.

"Corky, go lie down!" A woman with long, loose dark hair streaming down her back came down the steps. The dog retreated to his hideout with a last snarl, but Tye hardly noticed.

Dulcie. His eyes took in every detail of her appearance. She looked the same, yet not the same. Some-

thing in him still responded to the mere sight of her....
Simple chemistry, he told himself. Her hair was longer
and her eyes looked tired, strained. He thought she'd
gained a little weight, too, though the few extra
pounds didn't look bad. When he'd known her in Albuquerque, she'd been almost too slender. *Almost.*
His gaze lingered on her breasts, and he remembered
how beautiful they'd been in his palms the night she'd
come to him. His memory hadn't done them justice,
by the look of the full, soft mounds beneath her loose
shirt.

"Hey, Zed." Dulcie greeted the rancher through the
open window of the truck. "What brings you back
this way?"

"Got a delivery for you," the man drawled.

Dulcie's eyebrows rose and she cocked her head in
question. "A delivery...?"

Tye opened his door and swung his legs to the
ground, shouldering the duffel bag that was his only
luggage. The landscape swam in front of him for a
moment. He took a deep breath and rose, looking
across the bed of the truck at the woman he came to
see. "Hello, Dulcie."

Her face drained of color and she took a step backward. "Tye? What are you doing here?"

"I came to visit you." He walked around the truck
toward her but stopped when she took another step
back. She clearly wasn't pleased to see him, and he was
surprised at how bad that made him feel. He hadn't
known until just now how much he had counted on
her welcome, her smile. What was the matter with her?

The door opened again while Dulcie stood staring at him as if he had two heads. Tye glanced beyond her at the blond woman emerging from the house.

"Hey, Angel," Zed said from behind him. "I brought you a guest."

"A guest?" The blonde looked surprised, but her face lit in a gracious smile as she walked toward him and extended her hand. "Hello, I'm Angel Kincaid. Welcome to the Red Arrow."

Tye shook her hand. "Thank you. I'm Tye Bradshaw, a friend of Dulcie's."

The blonde turned to look curiously at Dulcie. "You didn't tell me you were expecting anyone."

"I wasn't." Dulcie's voice was low and expressionless.

What the hell was wrong with her? She knew as well as he did that it wasn't his fault that they'd been out of touch for so long. The pounding in his head was growing more and more insistent, and he knew from the times he'd been thrown by a horse and landed on his head that he'd better find a place to sit down before he passed clean out. "I wanted to surprise her," he said to Angel as he moved slowly around the truck. "We were next-door neighbors in Albuquerque." He was sweating with the effort it took to concentrate.

Angel frowned. "Are you well, Mr. Bradshaw?"

He attempted a smile. "I've been better. My car was broadsided by a pickup in Deming."

"Doctor wanted to keep him, but he wouldn't stay," said the helpful rancher from behind him. Zed extended a sheet of paper to Dulcie, who automatically reached for it. "Instructions," he said succinctly.

Dulcie heaved a sigh, apparently coming to some decision. "I guess you'll have to come in." She turned and began to lead the way to the house.

Tye followed her. He felt too lousy to ask her what her problem was. Later, when he felt better, he would tackle Dulcie.

As the rancher drove away, Angel followed them into the coolness of the house. All Tye could see of Dulcie was her rigid back, but he was aware of her silent disapproval every step of the way. He wondered if she was angry with him for leaving so abruptly after they'd . . . gotten together. He *had* tried to call her. He couldn't help it if she had never returned his messages. If she had— *What in hell was that noise?*

A baby. He'd spent enough time around his two cousins' families to recognize the sound of a baby squalling in outrage. His head pounded with each fresh shriek, and he put a hand to the wall to steady himself.

Dulcie gave a squeak of dismay. But it was Angel who darted ahead into the first room to the left, off the foyer they'd entered. The howling sound stopped abruptly. Tye stepped into what was obviously a living room to see Angel cradling a very small baby in her arms, gently patting its bottom and cooing at it. In the corner of the room, next to a massive timber-and-stone fireplace, was a bassinet in which the baby must have been sleeping.

"That's my little man. Did we go out and leave you all alone? You didn't like that one bit, did you?" As Angel spoke, the baby gradually quieted.

"Sit down." Dulcie pointed to a chair. Her voice was dull and devoid of warmth, her soft brown eyes unreadable.

He hesitated. He desperately wanted to talk to her, but the room was spinning around him and he couldn't quite focus on her face.

When he didn't immediately comply, she frowned. "You look like you're about to keel over. Will you please sit down?"

He sat. She was right. But he had to get her alone. Before he could say anything, though, she lifted her head from the doctor's instructions. "You have a concussion but you wouldn't stay for observation?"

"No way." He gingerly rolled his head in a negative motion against the high back of the chair where he'd collapsed. "I've had a concussion before. It'll pass. If I could just lie down . . . ?"

"In a minute," she said. "You also broke your finger. Did you at least let them treat that?"

Well, she wasn't fussing over him in quite the sympathetic way he'd imagined she might, but the note of concern in her voice could be taken as a positive sign. He hoped. "Yeah." He held up the splinted digit for her inspection. "They can't do much except straighten it out and wait for the bones to knit."

Dulcie nodded. Then she asked, "Can your car be repaired?"

"I think so. They said something about the frame probably being..." He just couldn't seem to retrieve the memory and instead fished a note out of his pocket, grimacing as the movement jarred his head. "They took it to this body shop and told me to call them tomorrow to see how long it will be."

Dulcie took the note and scanned it. "I'll call them later and tell them to put a rush on it. I guess you can stay here for a day or so until it's done."

So much for positive thinking.

"Dulcie!" Angel sounded rather startled, though she laughed to cover it. "We'll extend our hospitality as long as you need it, Mr. Bradshaw. By the way. I'm Dulcie's sister-in-law."

"Thank you. And make it Tye."

Angel had her hands full with the baby—it was squirming and squealing, banging its head against her chest repeatedly. "Are you getting hungry?" she said to the little one. "I'll give you to—"

"Why don't you change him before he eats?" Dulcie interrupted. "I'll show Tye to a room and get him an ice pack for that finger." To him, she said, "Follow me." And before he could protest, she swung his duffel bag across her shoulder and marched out of the room.

He thought Angel looked a bit confused, but the expression passed so quickly that he couldn't be sure. And the pounding in his head was growing worse by the second. Turning, he followed Dulcie up a staircase of pine and down a long, wide hallway flanked by at least half a dozen bedrooms. When she opened the door into a spacious guest room, he sank down immediately onto the handmade quilt that covered the big bed, with his booted feet dangling down over the edge.

With the same brisk efficiency the nurses at the hospital had shown earlier, she removed his boots and lifted his feet to the bed, all without uttering a word. Then she left him, to return a few moments later with an ice pack that he placed over his broken finger. It was swollen and rapidly turning an incredible shade of plum, but his head hurt too badly for it to bother him much.

"Get some rest," she said, and in her voice he heard the first note of compassion he'd noticed yet. He tried to take her hand, but she placed herself out of reach in a too-casual movement that briefly infuriated him.

"I will," he said, "and later we're going to talk."

She didn't answer, just slipped from the room and left him alone.

Tye closed his eyes and drifted, finally sleeping for a while. At one point, Angel came in and roused him briefly, checking his pupils and then leaving him to sleep some more.

Sometime later, he awoke again. He started to lever himself upright, but a sharp wave of pain in his hand left him gasping for a moment. When his disorientation had subsided, he remembered where he was—and why. With interest, he looked around the room. For all he knew, Dulcie could have decorated this.

The room was sparsely but attractively furnished, with a large, double-door wardrobe and a comfortable-looking chair made of pine the only furnishings other than the bed and adjacent table. A tall cactus in a ceramic pot stood in one corner, and painted deer-skin pillows were piled on both the bed and the chair. On the bedside table was a stocky candle in a copper holder, and near it was a round clock face set into the carved shape of a buffalo. The clock read 5:12, so he figured he'd been resting for about two and a half hours.

His stomach growled loudly. Dinnertime would be soon and he realized he'd missed lunch completely. He'd probably been in X ray through the noon hour, though he hadn't been aware of it at the time.

Thinking of the hospital reminded him of his physical state. He raised his hand and inspected the broken finger. Other than looking like a purple hot dog, it was fine. At least it didn't hurt as much anymore. If he didn't try to use it for anything.

Gingerly, he sat up, testing the state of his head as he pushed himself into a vertical position. A dull ache throbbed behind his eyes but the blinding pain was gone. Mentally he thumbed his nose at the doctor from the emergency room. *See? Told you I was fine. Growing up on a ranch makes a man tough. Got to be dead before I can be hospitalized.*

Still, it wasn't wise to push it too far, he thought. Prudently, he stuffed his toe into the top of one boot and dragged it toward him so that he could stomp into it without bending over. Then he repeated the process. Feeling pretty pleased with himself, he carefully rose, waiting for a mild wave of dizziness to pass before he walked out of the bedroom and headed for the staircase he dimly remembered coming up a few hours earlier.

What was Dulcie doing now? Recalling her behavior earlier, he realized that his chances of regaining her friendship—or anything else—were slim at this point. The idea didn't set well. Only, of course, because he hated to be at odds with his friends.

He started down the hallway toward the steps he'd come up a few hours ago, intending to hunt her down and make her talk to him. A sound from the far end of the hallway caught his attention and he paused at the top step. Somewhere back there a woman was humming. And it sounded enough like Dulcie's voice that he turned and retraced his steps, going past his bedroom and on down the hallway to the last door on the left.

The door was slightly ajar and the humming came from within. It was definitely Dulcie's voice. He'd heard her hum while she'd made a meal for him one evening in Albuquerque. Elated at the opportunity to speak privately with her so soon, he put a hand against the door and pushed lightly.

The door swung open.

Dulcie sat in a rocking chair, gazing down at the baby in her arms. Her blouse hung open and the infant was suckling greedily at her exposed breast.

Shock tore through him. *The child was hers!*

He must have made some sound, because Dulcie's head jerked up. A startled gasp escaped her, and her dark eyes widened to panicked proportions when she saw him standing there.

He couldn't move. Wild thoughts were chasing through his brain faster than he could examine them all. Observations battered at his senses: the barely visible crown of the baby's head covered in a down of dark hair... Dulcie's arm tenderly cradling the tiny child... one little hand kneading his mother's warm flesh as he suckled...

Finally, knowing he had questions that had to be answered, Tye took a deep breath and strode forward into the room where Dulcie and her baby sat.

His movement seemed to release her from stasis, as if she'd been frozen until then. She whipped a small blanket from the back of the rocking chair and draped it over her shoulder, arranging it to cover the nursing infant and her bare breast.

"What are you doing sneaking around like that?" Her face was as angry as her voice.

Dulcie's harsh demand seemed to frighten the baby; Tye saw its little legs jerk spasmodically, and then the child began to cry. Immediately, Dulcie's attention shifted. She drew the baby from beneath the blanket and cradled him in her arms, murmuring to him in low tones and gently patting his tiny back until gradually the infant quieted. After a moment, she placed him back under the blanket, frowning in concentration as she guided him to her breast.

The ease with which she handled the baby hammered home the truth that he was trying to deny, despite the clear evidence he'd seen. *This baby really was Dulcie's.*

Tye was stunned. His head had begun to throb again. Who was this child's father? At some point during those first days of getting to know each other in Albuquerque, he'd learned that Dulcie was separated from her husband, awaiting a divorce. At the time, Tye had thought Lyle Meadows must have been a blind man and a stupid one to boot.

But if the baby wasn't Lyle's... Despite the pain, his mind engaged in some rapid calculations. It had been almost exactly ten months ago that he and Dulcie had made love the first and only night they'd spent together. The same night that she'd discovered her husband's infidelity. If she had conceived then, and if she'd carried the child to term, the baby should be somewhere around a month old.

Cautiously, he cleared his throat, hoping his voice wouldn't betray his dismay. "How old is he?"

Dulcie raised her chin and traded him stare for stare.

He'd remembered her as a quiet woman, soft and soothing, easily managed. There was nothing of those qualities in her now. He held her gaze, silently willing her to drop hers first.

She continued to look straight into his eyes. "My son is three weeks old."

Three weeks old. The room swam around him again for a moment, but this time it wasn't because his head hurt. Dismay and shock combined in a force that was nearly a physical sensation, sucking the breath from his chest. *This was all his fault.*

He'd taken advantage of her.

Ten months ago, Dulcie Meadows had been vulnerable and alone. She'd come to him for comfort and understanding. Oh, he'd been comforting, all right. And he'd been as understanding as could be. But if he'd been a true gentleman, he would have backed away. He wouldn't have taken what she offered, would have realized that what she needed was a friend, not a horny fool like him.

Yet if he were completely honest, he was damned glad he wasn't a gentleman on that single night with Dulcie. The only thing he really regretted was the way they had parted. He'd meant to go after her, to talk to her when she'd calmed down, but the phone call from his uncle had changed everything, and he'd had to rush off to Montana without settling things with Dulcie.

Telling himself that he'd tried to get in touch with her was little consolation. The whole time he'd been taking care of Uncle Ike's ranch, he'd thought of her. He felt guilty and was determined to apologize.

That, of course, was what he'd made himself believe until now.

Until he'd seen her again.

But this...this wasn't the way he'd expected their reunion to go.

Rage began to rise, both at himself and at Dulcie. What a fool he'd been. In all these months, he had never considered that there might have been consequences resulting from their night together.

Consequences. What a stupid euphemism. A baby was a darn sight more than a "consequence." A baby was a huge, permanent obstacle in the simple path his life was following.

Why hadn't she told him she was pregnant? One thing was clear: she sure hadn't been thinking of him the way he'd constantly had her on his mind. God, if he hadn't followed her down here, he still wouldn't know that they'd created a baby together.

A baby. *His baby.* All his adult life he'd been careful to assume responsibility for birth control...until Dulcie. He'd vowed he would never have an illegitimate child, would never subject a child of his to the inevitable cruel taunts that would bring. All his life he'd been on the outside looking in at kids who belonged, kids who would never know how the word "bastard" could slice through a child's vulnerable heart. For he knew all too well how much that hurt.

And now he had a son who would bear the same stigma.

Dulcie sat frozen in the rocking chair, willing herself not to quail before the fury in Tye's incredulous gaze.

He swore quietly, viciously, and she flinched despite her best efforts.

Finally, he stopped and just stared at her again. "He's mine."

She was supremely conscious of the slurping, grunting sounds her son made as he suckled. Tye must have heard him, too, because his gaze dropped momentarily to the outline of the baby's body beneath the light throw she'd draped over herself. Superstitiously she crossed her fingers beneath the blanket.

"He's not yours. He's Lyle's."

"That's bull and you know it." Tye's voice was rough and tight. "A blood test will prove it, too."

"No!" She forced herself to mute the protest that escaped so that she wouldn't upset the baby. "I'm telling you this is my husband's child."

Tye snorted. "Not likely, darlin'. I seem to recollect you telling me in no uncertain terms that your marriage bed hadn't been used for anything besides sleep for a long time before I met you."

Oh, she could just die. She remembered exactly when that conversation had taken place. And from the way Tye's big body stilled and his nostrils flared, she knew he was recalling the same thing.

"Things happened after you left for Idaho—"

"Montana." It was a snarl.

"Montana, then. Lyle and I resumed—"

"You're lying. You expect me to believe you went back to that jerk after walking in on him in bed with another woman? I don't think so." The heavy scorn in his voice brought a rush of heat to her cheeks, but before she could formulate a response, he went on. "If it's true, then I'm sure good ol' Lyle won't mind telling me about it. Shall I track him down and give him a call?"

The heat drained from her cheeks as suddenly as it came and left her cold. Freezing. "No." She wanted to fight, to throw him out of her life, but she could see from the set look on his face that he wouldn't go. Closing her eyes in defeat, she laid her head against the back of the rocker. "Lyle was killed in an automobile accident shortly after the divorce."

Silence filled the room. When he didn't answer, she opened her eyes.

He looked shocked, and for a moment she was meanly pleased to have knocked him off stride. But before she could congratulate herself too much, Tye recovered his voice.

"I'm sorry. That must have been a jolt even though you weren't married any longer." His tone grew steely. "Still, it doesn't change anything, does it? That baby is mine and I'll do whatever I have to to prove it."

She didn't know what else she could say, so she said nothing, just lowered her head and watched her son's tiny feet flex as he tugged vigorously at her breast. Really, there was nothing more to say. If Tye forced the issue, he'd have no trouble finding out that he was indeed a father. She'd even listed him on the birth certificate.

Why had he come down here?

Even before she had learned of her pregnancy, she'd assumed she would never see him again. Truthfully, she hadn't wanted to. Her behavior on the night she'd caught Lyle having sex with another woman wasn't exactly something she wanted to recall.

She hadn't planned on telling Tye he was going to be a father, honestly hadn't thought he would want to know. In the few talks they had had about his photographic career, he had never hinted at any desire to settle down to family life. In fact, she distinctly remembered he'd said that bachelorhood suited him just fine. He'd been out of town half the time she had lived next to him. He was a wanderer, just like her husband had been. And she knew better than to expect anything from a wanderer.

Panic began to well up, clogging her throat with fear. What would happen now?

"Dulcie." His voice interrupted her racing thoughts.

She looked up and was captured in the full intensity of his golden eyes. She'd forgotten how compelling his eyes were, how beautiful. His driver's license called them hazel, but the word was only a pale description—

"Is this our baby?" His words were quiet and plaintive, demanding honesty.

She swallowed, unable to look into those eyes and lie any longer. "Yes."

A grimace twisted his face for a second.

It was gone so quickly that she couldn't decipher it. Was he angry? Or had that been pain she'd glimpsed?

"Why didn't you call me when you found out you were pregnant?" There was no accusation or demand in his voice, only bewilderment.

Dulcie shrugged, looking across the room at the copper-and-turquoise mobile that danced above the dressing table. "I didn't know how to reach you," she said.

Tye frowned and a small snort escaped him. "I slipped a note under your door with the number at my uncle's ranch the morning I left. And I tried to call

you, remember? Several times. Every time I did, I left
the number." He shook his head, looking at the baby
as if he couldn't fathom that it was real. "But you
never called me back."

Dulcie cleared her throat as she placed the baby
against her shoulder and began to rub his back. "I,
um, I didn't keep your number."

"You didn't . . ." His words trailed off.

She saw the anger flare again, saw the conscious effort he made to overcome what she had to admit was
a justified urge to shout at her. Why had she ever
thought she could or *should* raise her son without at
least giving his father the chance to know him?

"What's his name?" Tye stepped closer and
stretched out a finger, drawing back just before he ca-
ressed a tiny pink arm.

"Ryan." Dulcie was mesmerized by those eyes
again. Hadn't she always been? Even when they'd just
been friends, she'd been aware of his sex appeal. But
now, it filled the room, making her supremely aware
of the intimate bond they shared. "His name is Tyler
Ryan Kincaid. I took my maiden name back after the
divorce."

The small twitch at the corner of his eye was the
only sign he gave of his surprise, but his voice was
deadly quiet when he spoke. "You named him after
me, but you weren't going to tell me about him?"

Two

His son. Tye swallowed the lump that rose in his throat. *He had a son.*

Nothing in his life had prepared him for the emotion that surged through him as reality sank in. For a moment, all his misgivings were submerged beneath a growing sense of wonder.

He circled around to the side of the rocking chair to get a better look at the baby. The child's round skull was covered with thick black hair that stuck straight up. His tiny head lolled to one side and his eyes were half closed, his arms hanging limply over Dulcie's shoulder. He looked the very picture of satiation.

Gently, Tye slipped his index finger beneath the baby's palm. When Ryan reflexively clasped his hand around his father's finger, Tye smiled. "Wow. He's got quite a grip for such a little guy."

"He's not so little," she said. "He weighed over nine pounds when he was born."

His cousin Leslie's second daughter had been almost that big, and he remembered the horror story her husband told about how difficult the birth had been. He winced at the thought. Dulcie was small and petite, hardly built for delivering a miniature fullback. "Was it hard on you?"

She shrugged. "After twenty-three hours of labor, they thought I wasn't going to be able to deliver him. They were prepping me for a cesarean section when his head crowned and the doctor decided to give it one more try. I think it was about two more hours after that before he was delivered."

He was appalled. The thought of her suffering through a day of wrenching pain was more than he could bear to think about. "Were you alone?" he asked.

She shook her head. "Angel was with me." Then her lips curved into a wry smile. "Although I wish she hadn't been. That experience could have turned her off pregnancy for life."

He didn't share her mirth. "Dammit, Dulcie, I could have been there. I could have helped you." His voice reflected the bitterness that rose within him. "But you never gave me the chance. You were going to cut me out of my son's life without a second thought. Why?"

Her hand moved restlessly over the baby's back, and she wouldn't meet his eyes. "I...we really didn't know each other that well, Tye. You're devoted to your work and you're always traveling. I honestly didn't think it would matter to you." Her hand hesitated for a moment, and she looked up at him with an unspoken apology in her dark eyes. "Now I realize that was unfair."

"Unfair?" Tye snorted. "That's an understatement." He eased his finger from his son's tiny fist and walked across the room, massaging the back of his neck with one hand.

"What will you do now?" Behind him, Dulcie's voice was filled with apprehension.

He pivoted to face her. "How the hell do I know? I just found out I'm a father five minutes ago. I need some time to think about this." And just like that, he knew what he needed to do. "You and I have to talk, to make some decisions. I'll stay here at the ranch for a while until we can sort all this out."

Dulcie's eyes widened. "Here? In this house?"

"In this house," he confirmed. Seeing her brows draw together, he added, "And just in case you're thinking of refusing, let me remind you that I could take this to court if I have to. I have a right to be involved in my son's life."

Dulcie was silent for so long that he wondered what she was thinking. When she finally spoke, it wasn't the stinging response for which he'd braced himself. "What about your job?" she asked. "Don't you have to work?"

Tye thought of the healthy nest egg his free-lance photography had provided, about the way his agent was constantly pestering him to approve limited-edition prints from some of his work. "Let me worry about that," he advised her.

The ringing of the dinner bell interrupted any more conversation. He waited in the hall until Dulcie rearranged her clothing, then followed her downstairs to the dining room, where the table was prepared for dinner.

Three cowboys were taking seats as he entered. Dulcie pointed to a seat at the long table and told him, "Sit there." She placed Ryan in a little cradle next to the far corner of the table and took a seat where she could see the baby. Just then, Angel backed through the door from what he assumed was the kitchen. Behind her was a little girl with glossy, bouncing dark curls carrying a fistful of napkins, which she handed to Dulcie. Angel set a large casserole dish on the table and turned to lift the little girl into a chair. Another cowboy, easily the biggest man in the room, entered through the same door, carrying a huge bowl of baked potatoes, as well as a covered basket from which wafted the fragrant scent of bread. He set them on the table and took the seat at the head of the table, with Angel on his right and the child seated between them.

Angel placed her hand on the man's brawny forearm. "Day, we have a visitor this evening. This is Tye Bradshaw." She turned and smiled at Tye. "Tye, this is my husband, Day Kincaid, Dulcie's brother."

The rancher rose at the same time Tye did. The hand he extended met Tye's in a grip strong enough to crush bone. Tye returned it in full measure, not easing the pressure until Day grinned and relaxed his palm. "Welcome to the Red Arrow, Tye. What brings you to these parts?"

As both men resumed their seats, Dulcie rushed into speech before Tye could explain his presence. "Tye was my neighbor in Albuquerque. He's going to be visiting for a few days."

A few days? Tye turned his head and stared at Dulcie until she dropped her gaze to her plate. He had a suspicion it was going to take more than a few days to straighten out everything between them. When he looked at Day Kincaid again, the welcome had faded from Day's eyes and a guarded speculation had replaced his initial friendliness.

Angel carried on with the introductions. Tye saw her nudge her husband in the ribs with a surreptitious elbow, clearly a warning to mind his company manners. "Tye was involved in an accident in Deming, and his car is under repair." Then she turned to Tye again, naming for him the three cowhands who were grouped at the foot of the table. She finished by pointing to the little girl. "And this is our daughter, Beth Ann. She's a big help with her new cousin Ryan."

The child giggled and nodded vigorously. "I sing songs to Ry'n. He loves my songs."

Tye couldn't help grinning. The child reminded him of his two cousins' little girls. "How old are you, Beth Ann?" he asked.

She proudly held up four stubby fingers. "Fou'."

"Wow!" He feigned amazement. "I have two little nieces the very same age."

Beth Ann looked fascinated. "What's 'ere names?"

"Melody and Ariel," he answered. "Melody has a big sister named Pamela and Ariel has two baby sisters called Margaret and Katie." When he glanced at Dulcie, there was a speculative expression on her face, and he didn't trust the gleam in her eye.

"That's a lot of girls," she remarked. "I don't remember hearing about your family before."

No one else at the table could have registered the dig but Tye. Hell! He hadn't purposely concealed anything from Dulcie. When they'd gone out together in Albuquerque, they'd talked only in generalities. Or about her marriage.

"Technically, they aren't my nieces, they're my cousins. I don't have any sisters or brothers," he said. No time like the present to start overcoming past mistakes. "Those are the children of the two cousins I was raised with."

He could see in her face the desire to question him further, but the rest of the company gathered around the table inhibited her.

"So you're from Albuquerque?" Dulcie's brother addressed him from the end of the table.

Tye shook his head. "Not originally. And not recently. My family is in Montana. I'm a free-lance photographer, and for a while I had an apartment in Albuquerque." He inclined his head toward Dulcie. "Which is where Dulcie and I met. But I've spent the

last year on a Montana cow-calf operation, working
for my uncle after he fell and shattered his left leg
pretty badly.''

Day's eyes lit up. "How many head?"

The rest of the meal was dominated by ranch talk.
Although Tye could tell Day hadn't forgotten to be
suspicious of him, Tye liked Dulcie's brother. And her
sister-in-law, Angel. A beautiful woman. Idly he
wondered what there was about human attraction that
made him only mildly interested in her undeniable fair
beauty, while every cell in his body was alert to Dulcie's presence when she was in the room. No way could
he pretend he was indifferent to Dulcie.

That was good, Tye decided as he watched his son's
tiny body stretch and squirm as Ryan awoke from his
catnap in the cradle, because he was going to be seeing a lot of her in the future since they would be raising their son together. Together. The word brought a
whole host of interesting possibilities to mind, but he
pushed them aside to consider a more mundane matter.

He wanted to be involved in his son's life. Not just
hovering on the periphery but to be there on a daily
basis. There to witness the first step, the first word, to
set him on his first pony and to teach him to ride and
rope. Even more important, he wanted Ryan to have
the stability of a family of his own, to know he was
loved, to feel that he was special.

He knew what it was like to spend your life wondering what had been more important to your parents

than the child they had created and abandoned. Ryan was never going to have to face that.

He and Dulcie had created Ryan. For the rest of their lives they would be tied by that bond. He might as well admit it—there was only one conclusion to the thoughts racing around in his head. He was going to marry her.

Amazingly, the thought didn't bother him. He'd avoided commitment like the plague all his life because he hadn't thought he'd ever want the responsibility of children, and everybody knew marriage nearly always meant kids. But in the few short hours since he'd been presented with his son's existence, he'd been touching on the idea like a skittish colt who wanted sugar but was afraid of the hand that held it. Coming close, dancing away, drawing near again but not quite able to complete the leap of faith it took. Well, he guessed he was leaping now.

He couldn't imagine marriage to another woman, but marrying Dulcie seemed like a good idea to him. He'd spent enough time with her to know that she soothed him rather than irritated. And God knew they were a good match in bed.

The mere pairing of "bed" and "Dulcie" in the same thought was all it took to bring back vivid memories of the night she'd lain with him. Too vivid. He shifted in his seat and deliberately transferred his gaze to the squirming infant she was lifting from the pine cradle.

Ryan might be the reason for the marriage, but the more he thought about it, the better the idea seemed.

Then, when he was away on assignment, Ryan still would have one parent and a lot of support and stability in his life.

"Come into my study? I'd like to talk a little more."

Dulcie's brother was looking at him expectantly, and he realized Day had been addressing him. The man clearly was used to giving orders and having people jump.

Slowly, he pushed away his plate and rose. "The meal was delicious. Thank you."

Angel smiled graciously as she began to clear away the supper dishes. Dulcie avoided his eyes, but she looked worried about something. He promised himself that as soon as he could get away from Day, he'd talk to her some more.

He followed the other man toward the front of the house and into an office.

"Have a seat."

The tone in Day's voice wasn't an invitation but an order. What the hell was up here? Tye ignored the command, leaning against a sturdy bookshelf and consciously adopting a relaxed pose. "Thanks, I'll stand." He looked at the computer equipment spread across the desk. "What software do you use for your breeding program?"

"I didn't bring you in here to compare work techniques," Day said. His teeth clicked together audibly over the last word. "You're upsetting my sister. Angel told me Dulcie wasn't expecting you."

"She didn't know I was coming," he admitted. "I thought I'd drop in and see her while I was down this way."

"You'll have to leave tomorrow," Day said abruptly. "She's a new mother and a recent widow. She needs rest and no disruptions."

"I'm aware of Dulcie's needs. But she and I have some catching-up to do. I planned on a longer visit."

Day's face darkened. "My sister has had enough man trouble in her life to last her quite a while. If you're courtin', she's not interested."

Damn. He should have known this wasn't going to be easy. There was no help for it but to tell the truth. "I'm not exactly courtin'." He hesitated, then took a deep breath. "I'm Ryan's father. And I'm hoping to stay awhile."

The bald words ricocheted off every wall in the room. A second crawled by, then two. From the kitchen, the clatter of dishes seemed abnormally loud. Day's face would have made a great photograph, if Tye was into portraits. He'd title it *Shock Absorbing*.

"Is that true?" Day's sharp demand wasn't aimed at him. Tye turned, seeing for the first time that Dulcie stood behind him in the doorway.

She nodded, apparently speechless, but he could read pure outraged anger in her expression.

"But... what about Lyle...?" Day was floundering, apparently trying to figure out how to phrase his questions in a delicate manner. At any other time, Tye would have found his efforts immensely amusing.

"Tye and I weren't . . . we didn't . . . we were just friends until my divorce was final," Dulcie informed her brother in a steely tone. "Not that it's any of your business."

Good for her. Intent on Dulcie, Tye never saw the fist that connected with his jaw. He didn't even get his hands out in time to break the fall, and Day's punch knocked him flat on his back on the hard wooden floor.

He lay there, his head throbbing. The headache from the accident that had been held at bay after his nap returned in force. He was seeing three and four of everything, but his hearing was unimpaired and he had no trouble deciphering the raw fury beneath the blistering curses that Day Kincaid was heaping on his head.

"Get up," Day said through his teeth. "Get up so I can knock you down again. You're not fit to lick my sister's boots. It might be okay in Montana to use a woman without worrying about consequences, but around here we do things differently. Real men don't leave their women to face pregnancy and birth alone. Real men don't father bas—"

"Day, stop it!" The command was a harsh scream. "He's injured. You might have done permanent damage to his head." Dulcie was kneeling at Tye's side, her fingers gently exploring the spot on his jaw where Day's fist had landed.

Day uttered a growl of contempt. "I figure that would be an improvement." He glared at Tye. "Get up."

Tye climbed to his feet, despite Dulcie's protests. He still saw two of the furious dark-haired man, but he did his best to focus on one of them. "You can pound on me some more if it makes you feel better. I probably deserve it." He paused, then looked at Dulcie, holding her gaze with his own as he spoke to her brother. "But I won't fight back. Dulcie's already too upset. She needs rest and relaxation right now. Having the two of us at each other's throat won't help."

Dulcie's big brown eyes were fastened on his face. Though he was speaking to her brother, he was communicating with her, as well. *I'm sorry. Let me try to make this right.*

Day cleared his throat.

Dulcie shook her head slightly, as if she was coming out of a trance. Her expression darkened again as she stomped across the room toward Day. "How dare you!"

"Huh?" Day looked taken aback by her attitude. "What did I do?"

"I can fight my own battles." Dulcie shook her finger in his face, so close that he flinched and blinked. "Stop pretending to be a protective older brother."

"I'm not pretending." Day's tone was injured.

"I know." Dulcie's voice softened slightly. "And it's nice to know you care. But I can straighten out my life without any interference from you." She slipped behind him and gave him a hefty shove that barely succeeded in jostling his solidly muscled frame. "Now go away. Tye and I need to talk."

"All right. But I want to say one last thing to lover boy here." Day looked back over Dulcie's head at Tye. "I'm not sorry I hit you. And if you want to try a re-match, you just name the date."

"Out!" Dulcie stomped her foot and flung out an arm toward the door.

With a last unreadable glance at his sister, Day left the room.

When the door closed behind him, Dulcie turned to face Tye. Or maybe turned *on* him was more accu-rate, he decided. The woman didn't look happy. Even so, she was enchanting.

Her glossy black hair curled wildly to a point below her shoulders, and her dark eyes were sparkling with temper. Her brows were drawn together in a manner that she probably thought looked ferocious, but to him only emphasized her fragility and femininity. He'd been attracted to her quiet, self-contained beauty in Albuquerque, but he'd sensed there was more to her than she would share with him. Perhaps that had been part of her charm.

Now he was seeing what lay below the surface. And far from boring or repulsing him, he found this new, spirited woman more exciting than ever.

"And *you*," she said in a tone laden with fury. "How dare you talk about me behind my back? If I'd wanted Day to know you were Ryan's father, I would have told him myself."

That stung. Already he was absurdly proud of his newfound parent status. "You should have told him," he said harshly. "Just like you know in your heart you should have told me."

That stopped her. Dulcie paused with her mouth open to deliver another verbal blast, and to his chagrin, he saw tears rising in her eyes. "This won't work," she said. "You're going to have to leave."

He would have gone to her and taken her in his arms, but she dragged her sleeve across her eyes and he realized her temper hadn't abated. Instead, he crossed his arms and shook his head. "Nope."

"But I can't *think* when you're around." She crossed the floor to him and placed her hand on his arm. "Please, Tye. Each of us needs to have time to decide what we want for Ryan before we try to discuss it. I won't try to exclude you anymore. I just don't want to make any rash decisions."

She looked so appealing that he couldn't prevent himself from unfolding his arms and sliding his uninjured hand up to cup her elbow. Drawing her closer, he slipped his arms around her shoulders and dropped his head to nuzzle his nose in her soft hair. "I don't need time," he murmured. "I know exactly what I want for our son."

"And what's that?" she whispered. She held herself rigid and unyielding, but her breathing was shallow and uneven and her breath was warm against his throat. The tips of her breasts brushed his chest over and over again. He had to restrain himself from yanking her to him so that he could feel every womanly curve again.

But he didn't want to spook her. And truthfully, he didn't feel good enough right now for a serious advance. He wanted to do this right. Tye kissed her ear, then began to trail his lips along her temple. The blood was pulsing through his body in a stirring tempo heightened by her proximity. "I'm prepared to marry you."

She stood frozen for a moment, but he'd expected some initial shock and he kept up the lightly sensual caresses. In a minute she'd think it through and be relieved. Maybe she would even be glad—

"You're *prepared* to marry me?" Her voice was strident and filled with fury as she tore herself out of his embrace, and he realized that she wasn't reacting in quite the way he'd anticipated.

"Yes." She should be pleased, shouldn't she? It was important that Ryan have a father in his life. And legitimacy. That was important, too.

"You're prepared to marry me." This time it wasn't a question but a statement loaded with sarcasm. "What a lucky girl I am." Her eyes narrowed as she surveyed Tye from head to toe and back again with insulting thoroughness.

"Look..." He didn't know what to say to reassure her. "We've both made mistakes. But I'd like to correct them. I can provide for you and Ryan, if that's part of the problem here." He knew he sounded defensive, but he couldn't figure out why she seemed to be so mad now.

"Marriage to you isn't going to correct anything," Dulcie said emphatically. "I don't need you to provide for Ryan and me. I have a family and work right here on the ranch. You, on the other hand, travel constantly. I have no intention of marrying another man who plunks me in an apartment somewhere and takes off for weeks on end.''

"You know my schedule is flexible. We could work something out.'' Although he couldn't think of anything workable right at the moment.

"How would I know your schedule is flexible?'' Her voice rose. "I don't know anything about your work! You take pictures…and that's all you've ever told me. Pictures of what? Something that requires travel, obviously.''

He hesitated. His work was a private thing, always had been. Not even his family in Montana knew how well he'd done for himself. It wasn't something he'd consciously planned. It was more that he'd felt separate, not quite a part of a family unit for as long as he could remember. He knew he was like a son to Uncle Ike and Aunt Gem, like a brother to their two daughters, but he'd always felt in his heart that he didn't really belong.

His photography was the only way he'd ever found to define himself, to identify himself without needing the context of family to tell him who he was. He was proud of what he'd accomplished, proud of who he was. And if he wanted to create a family with Dulcie, he supposed he'd have to share that with her.

He crossed to Day's desk, silently pointing to the cover of a glossy stock journal on the corner.

Dulcie raised an eyebrow. "What?''

"This is mine." He could remember the day he'd taken the photo like it was yesterday. He'd waited for two hours in the hot sun for that Brangus bull to look his way. Finally, he'd begun to throw small pebbles to attract the dozing animal's attention. It had worked a little too well. When the bull had spotted him, he'd not only looked but charged. It wasn't the first time in Tye's life that he'd been charged or chased, but it was the first that he'd ever vaulted a fence running uphill wearing more than a dozen pounds of camera equipment.

But Dulcie didn't look very impressed. "You take pictures of cattle?"

"Among other things." He shrugged. "I've been described as a photographer of 'the Western way of life.'"

"And magazines pay you for that?"

"Yep." He hesitated, then figured he'd better let her hear it all. "I've sold prints to collectors and had two coffee-table books published. Dulcie, money is not a problem. I'm more than able to take care of you and Ryan. You wouldn't have to work."

"That's not why I asked." Her voice was still acid. "You know a lot about me, but in the time we knew each other, you never shared anything about yourself. All I was to you was a warm body—" her voice rose "—and that's no basis for marriage. So stop feeling guilty about me, cowboy. I wouldn't marry you if you made a million bucks a year!"

She started past him, clearly planning a grand exit with the last word, but his temper, usually so even, snapped beneath the contempt in her tone.

He grabbed her arm and dragged her to a halt, shoving his face close to hers, ignoring the startled shock in her eyes. "Don't think we're done with this discussion," he snarled. "I know all about how it feels to grow up as a bastard with no father, and my son is never going to be deprived that way!"

"Ryan is *not* a bastard!" she shouted back, yanking herself away. "And don't you ever think that he'll be deprived in any way. I did a fine job carrying him and bearing him alone, and I can do just fine raising him alone."

He winced as her sudden movement jolted a shaft of pain through his damaged finger, then closed his eyes and took a deep breath, forcing himself to calm down and find something soothing to say to her—

The door slammed.

His eyes flew open and he groaned, putting a hand to his throbbing head. She was gone. He could hear her quick, agitated footsteps receding along the hall for a minute, but the room spinning around him claimed his attention and he dropped to his knees on the study floor.

Guess his timing wasn't so great. Apparently, Dulcie didn't see marriage to him as the sensible solution that he thought it was. When he felt better, he'd try to talk to her again. *If* he ever felt better. Right now, about the only thing he was sure of was that he'd like to detach his head and set it on a shelf for a few days.

* * *

She'd have sworn this mattress hadn't been so lumpy yesterday. Dulcie turned over restlessly once more, resolutely ignoring the glowing numbers of her bedside clock. She already knew it was late.

For the past several hours, she hadn't been in this bed, on this ranch.

No, she'd been several hours and many miles north of here. Once again, with the startling clarity reserved for memories of profound shock, she'd walked into the tiny living room of the Albuquerque apartment she shared with her husband, Lyle. Or at least, it was the home where she'd lived while Lyle was jetting around the country wheeling and dealing the way he insisted a successful businessman had to if he wanted to make it in a competitive market.

The apartment had begun to feel like a prison as her marriage unraveled. Finally, after a last huge blowup, when she'd faced the fact that her marriage was over, she'd gone home. Back to the Red Arrow, where she was needed, where she was loved.

But just as she had begun to see that life didn't end with divorce, Lyle had called. Granted, he said he'd phoned to tell her that the divorce papers should be ready for her signature within the week, but it was what he didn't say that brought her back to Albuquerque. Lyle had sounded...what? Lonely? Perhaps. Depressed? That, too. There had been some indefinable poignancy in his voice, in the way he'd simply hung on the line as if he had just needed to hear her....

And in that drawn-out, hesitant moment, all her rage, all the animosities that had built between them as a result of his frequent and protracted absences vanished as she remembered the way it had been when they first met. Was he sorry things had come to this? Was there still a chance that they could salvage their love and their life together?

She didn't know.

And that was what took her back to the apartment that last time. She could never forgive herself if she walked out of her marriage without doing everything she could to preserve it. Marriage was a process of give and take. Maybe she hadn't given enough. Maybe Lyle was having some of the very same thoughts.

The apartment door was locked when she arrived in the early evening. Good thing her husband got home so late—she'd have time to clean the place and fix dinner. When the lock clicked and the door smoothly opened, she walked into the living room, tossing her purse on the hall table. Absently she noted that Lyle must be home, after all—his briefcase lay in the middle of the living room floor. It struck her as odd, considering what a freak about neatness and order he'd always been, but she was too intent on her mission to really notice. Maybe it was better this way—more spontaneous. If she had too much more time to think about what she wanted to say, she'd have it so mixed up she'd never get it out.

Rounding the corner into the hallway, she headed past the kitchen and dining areas, eager to find Lyle. A cursory glance showed no one in the kitchen, and she started to move on, but then she looked farther, at the small pine table tucked into the nook.

And she stopped, riveted in a shocked horror that froze her into immobility.

Lyle stood in front of the table, between the legs of a woman who was reclining on her elbows, her long hair streaming down as her head drooped backward. She was naked from the waist down and the tailored blouse beneath her suit jacket was unbuttoned and shoved to her sides, baring her breasts. Lyle's pants sagged around his ankles as the thighs of the woman on the table gripped his hips. His hands were on her breasts, kneading in rhythm with his thrusting hips. Amazingly, the pair were almost totally silent. Dulcie could nearly hear her own breathing.

She could definitely hear the hitching sob she sucked in as the scene before her seared into her brain.

The woman's head jerked upright. Dulcie would never forget the look of shock and panic on her flushed face. Nor would she ever forget what had happened next.

She had run from the apartment, disregarding Lyle's shouts for her to wait. The tears had blinded her even before she'd grabbed her purse and opened the door.

She probably would have jumped into her car and driven straight back to the ranch if Tye hadn't come down the hallway just then. He'd been a neighbor and a friend during her life in Albuquerque, and seeing his tall figure striding toward her had been a sweet relief. She knew Tye would help her.

Alone in the dark New Mexico night, she cried aloud. Oh, Tye had helped her, all right. And a few weeks later, the ink barely dry on her divorce decree, she'd realized she was pregnant with Tye's child.

Dulcie sighed and twisted to her other side again. Seeing him again had awakened all the illicit thoughts and memories she'd suppressed since she'd fled from his bed. Oh, she was wicked. Tye couldn't be blamed for anything. Everything that had happened with Tye that night was nobody's fault but her own. She'd practically begged him to take her, and she'd reveled in every minute of the rough, wild loving they'd shared. Just thinking about the way they had frantically shed each other's clothing, hands and mouths racing, sliding, tasting, gliding.... And the way he had taken control as he'd urged her atop him and mastered her with his big, hard body, telling her in hoarse whispers how beautiful she was and how much he'd wanted her, the way her body had accepted the heavy, surging demand of his....

Oh, yes, indeed, she was wicked. And she was driving herself crazy thinking about him. She should be sleeping while the baby was, for heaven's sake, not lying here getting herself all hot and bothered about a man who had only tracked her down because he thought he'd needed to apologize.

What a shock Ryan must have been to him! She could almost smile when she recalled the stunned look on his face earlier, seeing her nursing her son. Another more recent memory slipped into her mind, and she let it surface, examining her new knowledge from every angle, trying to make it fit with the man she knew.

Tye had said he knew about growing up a bastard. At the time, she'd taken him literally. Was that indeed what he had meant? And how might being an illegitimate child affect Ryan? Until now, she'd managed to avoid thinking about it, but she'd always been one to face unpleasantness head-on and get it over with. Would he be teased by other children? Called hateful names? Would he mind not having a father? She knew her brother Day would be more than happy to be a father to her son, but what about Ryan's feelings? Would his uncle Day be enough, or would there always be a part of him that longed for a daddy of his own?

With angry determination, she flipped back to the other side again, pulling the light quilt firmly around her shoulders. Weighing the pros and cons of providing Ryan with a stand-in for a father was futile now that Tye knew he had a son. She just knew he wasn't going to give up and go away quietly.

Three

Tye sat up and reached for the bottle of pain medication beside the lamp, downing two pills with the glass of water he'd set there before he went to bed. He'd rather be thrown from a bull than be in an auto accident, he decided. At least coming off a bull, he had the chance to prepare for the fall. As it was, he had aches and bruises in parts of him he'd never known he had before.

Something had wakened him, he thought. Some sound that hovered just outside his consciousness now, interfering with his need to get back to sleep. He held his breath and listened intently.

After a moment, the night sounds sorted themselves out: the upright clock at the end of the hallway steadily passing the seconds, the hoot of an owl somewhere out near the barn, the rhythmic creak of a floorboard—

That was it. The sound that didn't fit. He let out the breath he'd been holding and sucked in another one, held it again. There! The funny little squeak was what had wakened him. This time, a woman's low voice responded, soothing the small squeaker.

Dulcie. And the baby—Ryan. His gaze shifted to the clock. Wow. He hadn't really thought about it, but this was probably a nightly routine for Dulcie now. He knew from hearing his cousins talk that infants often took night feedings for several months. No wonder Dulcie looked exhausted.

No, he corrected himself, she didn't just look exhausted. She looked bone-deep weary and worn. And it was his fault.

As he looked back, it seemed impossible that nearly a year had passed since she'd come running into his arms in that hallway. She'd been in his thoughts so much while he'd been in Montana that it seemed a much shorter time.

But it hadn't been. And Ryan was living proof. Why in hell hadn't she told him she was expecting?

Why in hell didn't you try harder to track her down right away? Missing her pregnancy and Ryan's birth was his own stupid fault. He'd known just how upset Dulcie had been when they'd parted. He'd had a feeling when he couldn't get in touch with her again that she'd gone home to her family's ranch near Deming. And if he were honest with himself, hadn't he been hoping that she would miss him enough to call?

It still stung his ego when he remembered that she'd deliberately discarded the phone number he'd left her. That night had been something special to him. He could see why it might hold some less pleasant memories for her, but he guessed he needed to believe that she'd been as deeply affected by him as he had by her... deeply enough, maybe, to forget about that damned weasel of a husband she'd had.

Dulcie's husband. Tye's right fist flexed in response to the memory of the man, and he smiled grimly. When Lyle Meadows had knocked on his door after Dulcie had caught him cheating on her, Tye hadn't bothered to restrain himself. The jerk hadn't even stopped to pull his clothes together and he was still stuffing his shirt into his pants while he demanded to see his wife. But Tye considered that he'd been pretty low-key until the guy tried to shove him aside and enter Tye's apartment, where he'd taken Dulcie....

"You hit him!" There was an unholy delight in Dulcie's tone. "You actually hit him."

Tye nodded, smiling, unable to resist her glee. "Something crunched. I might have broken his nose."

Her eyes narrowed to slits that burned with dark fires of renewed rage. "Good! He deserved it. To think that I was actually feeling like I'd made a mistake. I drove up here today to tell him that I wanted to give our marriage another try. I was going to cook dinner, but then I thought he was already home and—"

She stopped abruptly and took a deep, gulping breath as her eyes filled with tears. All the steam drained out of her, and he could almost see her deflate as sorrow and humiliation began to crash over her head.

"Hey, woman," he said, taking her by the arms and leading her over to his couch. "Don't fall apart on me now."

"I'm sorry, Tye," she said, swiping at the tears that ran freely down her face. "It was just such a shock..." Her voice trailed away as she started to sob quietly, stuffing a fist against her mouth as if she could prevent the hoarse sounds from escaping.

He couldn't stand it. "Come here," he said, reaching for her. He hauled her into his lap and she burrowed against him, shoving her tear-streaked face into his neck. He could feel her slim frame shaking, and the force of her grief tore at him. Helplessly, he rubbed her back over and over again, rocking her slightly in an instinctive comforting gesture.

How long did he hold her? He didn't know, but he knew he'd remember what had happened afterward until the day he died.

Finally, she cried herself dry and began to stir in his arms. He let her go reluctantly, aware that their casual, neighborly friendship hadn't prepared either of them for the emotional intimacy of this situation. Up till today, the most personal thing they'd discussed was what topping they liked on their pizza.

Well, that wasn't altogether true. Once, when they'd gone to a movie together, he'd asked her if she got lonely while her husband was away. Her reply had been a single, wistful "Yes." He hadn't been able to figure out what to say to that, so he hadn't said any-thing, but after that, he'd made a point of spending some time with her whenever he was in town. From time to time after that day, she had discussed her marriage with him, but until now, it had always been in the abstract.

Now, it was painfully real.

Now, he was suddenly acutely aware of her weight in his lap, the soft slide of her bottom across him as she moved away and turned to face him.

"I apologize for making a scene," she said, "and for dragging you into my problems."

"Nothing to apologize for," he replied.

"Yes, there is." She picked up his right hand and brushed her thumb across his knuckles, which were slightly red and swollen. Then, before he could react, she lifted his hand to her lips and pressed a gentle kiss there.

"Thank you," she whispered, looking up at him with her open mouth still against the back of his hand.

The blatantly sexual gesture wasn't lost on him, and he squirmed uncomfortably, trying to disguise the leaping response of his flesh before she noticed how turned on he was getting. "It's all right," he said gruffly. "After the way he treated you, I kind of en-joyed it."

She smiled at him, and he swore there was an invi-tation in the rich depths of her eyes. "I haven't told you how much our times together have meant to me."

That was innocent enough. Surely she only meant that he'd been a good friend. But when she placed her slender hand on his thigh and squeezed lightly, he knew he wasn't imagining things.

Hell.

He'd been lusting after her perfect little body for months without really expecting anything would ever come of it, just because he was a man and she was a beautiful, beautifully made woman. He'd have to be crazy to turn her down.

But it wasn't right. He knew sex wasn't what she needed right now, even if she didn't. He could feel himself starting to sweat as he cupped her face in his hands and forced her to look at him.

"Dulcie...I don't want you to have any regrets about anything that goes on between us—"

"I won't." She caught his wrist with her free hand and drew it onto her breast. Onto her breast! He was still in shock at that sensation when he realized her other hand had crept up his thigh to the crease between his leg and his torso, where her thumb was gently tracing a path deeper and deeper into some very dangerous territory.

He almost choked on his own tongue trying to get out the words to stop her.

He'd tried. Honest to God, he really had. But she'd been like a miniature octopus, with too many arms for him to capture all at once. Twice more he'd protested, and her husky laughter had been one more nail in the coffin that confined his better judgment, her hands and her mouth speeding over him, eluding him, firing a rising tide of sexual arousal that in the end, he'd been unable to stem.

He'd taken her beneath him there, on his couch, and made her his in the most basic way there was. And when he'd dozed off and woken to find her astride him, he'd taken her again. And yet again, until they'd both been too exhausted to do anything but snuggle into the limited space and sleep.

When he'd awakened in the morning, she was gone.

His body throbbed now, remembering the hot, electric loving they'd shared. He hadn't had a woman since, partly because he'd been called home to Montana and he'd been working like a dog for the past year, and partly because his body simply couldn't be bothered to respond to any other female.

Thank God he'd found her. He forced himself to relax, muscle by muscle, until he was reasonably calm, but when sleep finally claimed him again, he dreamed of her.

The alarm clock wakened him. He couldn't remember what he had planned for the day, but he knew the horses needed attention. His arm shot out from beneath the covers to silence the alarm, but his groping hand couldn't find it. He sat up, disoriented and shivering in the predawn gloom, just as the alarm clock was shut off somewhere in another room.

For a moment, he drew a panicky blank as he looked around the unfamiliar room. Then a sound pierced the dawn and memory flooded back.

As it did, he was on his feet, moving out into the hallway. His head swam for a moment, but he stopped and waited and after a moment, he felt better. Not even a headache. Halfway down the hallway, he realized he was wearing nothing but the boxer shorts he slept in, but he didn't stop. He had a son to see.

Ryan was getting louder now, the first small squeaks of awakening beginning to escalate into infant outrage at being unattended. The door next to the room where Ryan slept was ajar, and he glanced in as he passed it. Then he stopped and looked again.

Dulcie lay on her stomach in the double bed, her face buried in pillows. All he could see was a wild cloud of glossy hair. She didn't even stir, and he thought again of how tired she'd looked. The baby's cries were increasing in volume now, and he wanted to reach Ryan before he woke up his exhausted mom.

Tearing himself from her doorway, he entered the nursery and stepped to the side of the crib. Ryan lay on his back, tiny feet and fists punching the air in impotent ire.

"Hey there, cowboy," Tye said softly. "What's the trouble?"

Ryan stopped hollering and looked at his father, apparently startled by the voice. After a moment, though, his little face screwed up to cry again.

Tye hesitated. He hated to have Dulcie wake so early if all the little guy wanted was some attention. Reaching into the crib, he slid one hand under Ryan's head and the other under his torso and lifted him.

Supporting the baby in front of him, Tye inspected his son. Ryan stared right back, his huge eyes already so dark that Tye could see they were going to be brown like his mother's. "Hey, cowboy," he said. "Are you gonna be an early riser?"

Ryan squirmed, his little legs pedaling as if he were riding a bicycle.

Tye grinned. "Oh, so you like the sound of your daddy's voice, do you?"

Ryan squirmed some more and Tye laughed aloud. "You're really something, you know that? I'm damned glad I showed up when I did, 'cause I might have missed all this."

Ryan had stopped crying while she was fumbling into her robe. Dulcie almost ran the few feet from her room to the doorway of the nursery, imagining all sorts of horrible reasons for the sudden silence.

But as she reached her son's room, she stopped in the doorway, surprised by the sight of Tye holding Ryan in front of him. Tye was naked except for his underwear—she couldn't take her gaze off the broad bronzed expanse of his shoulders and back, the muscular calves and long, solid thighs that disappeared beneath the small swatch of fabric. He was all man. She'd been imagining his body for ten long months; to have it thrown in her face first thing in the morning was simply too much. Her breath grew short and her breasts, already sensitive, tingled.

The tingling sensation was what saved her. She knew from experience what that signaled. Regardless of whether it was Ryan's suckling stimulating her letdown reflex or the sight of his nearly nude father, it didn't really matter. Crossing her arms over her breasts, she pressed hard, willing the moment to pass.

Tye was oblivious to her presence, laughing every time Ryan kicked his feet. He was talking to their baby, and she didn't miss the rapt look on Ryan's face at the sound of his father's voice. Of course he looked at everyone like that right now, she reasoned.

But from deep inside her, a feeling of helplessness rose. Ryan had been hers, and hers alone, for almost a year now, from the moment she'd first suspected she was pregnant until yesterday when Tye had walked back into her life. Now everything was going to have to change, and she didn't think she was ready for that.

And just exactly how would everything change? Tye wanted—no, *expected* her to marry him. He had to be crazy! They barely knew each other.

But a vivid image of just how well they did know each other rose in her mind and she felt herself blush. Still, that wasn't enough, she reminded herself sternly. Once before she'd married a man about whom she'd known little more than that they shared a mutual attraction, and look how that had turned out.

Be real, Duls, said an inner voice. *The way Lyle made you feel was nothing but a teaser compared to the way being with Tye is.* Tye made her feel like a quivering mass of nothing but need, a pile of dry tumbleweed just waiting for a lightning strike to send it burning everything in its path.

And that wasn't good. She didn't like it one bit, feeling so...so *needy.* She had to keep a clear head. She had to be the one to remind him that marriage between them was another name for disaster. She ought to know. She'd been married to a traveling man already.

Tye wouldn't be around for Ryan's childhood even if she did marry him. And how good would it be for her son to have a daddy blow in for a few days and then just about the time he was starting to depend on him, leave again?

Are you talking about Ryan or yourself?

It didn't matter. It didn't matter one bit how Tye made her feel. She still wasn't going to marry him, and she wasn't going to fool around with him anymore, either. She couldn't take that. Nope, she'd just have to ignore this *need* until it went away.

"Good morning." Deliberately, she waited in the doorway for Tye to see her.

"Hey, there." He turned and walked toward her, offering the baby to her. "I was hoping to let you get a little more sleep but I guess mothers are on some kind of internal timer."

She didn't reach for Ryan, though she was longing to snatch him and cuddle his sweetness to herself. "If you're going to be a daddy, you might as well learn how to change a diaper."

Tye's gaze held hers. "Am I going to be a daddy?"

She shrugged. "I can't stop you. We'll just have to work together to do what's best for Ryan."

To Tye's credit, he could have pressured her about marriage again, but he let the moment pass as she led the way to the changing table.

Laying Ryan on the padded surface, he said, "I've changed my nieces before, but I don't know much about little boys. Are there any tricks to this?"

She had to smile. "There's only one rule I religiously follow. Never leave that little water pistol uncovered unless you want to get squirted!"

Tye looked down at his son with new respect. "That's a nasty trick, cowboy. You wouldn't do that to your daddy, would you?" All the same, she noted that as he competently cleaned and changed the baby, he was careful to take her warning seriously.

His big hands looked far too large and clumsy to be handling Ryan's tiny body with such ease; she recalled how large and tanned his hands had looked against her skin so many months ago. *No!* She wouldn't think about that night. Surely she had more willpower than this.

She focused on Tye's hands again. They were just hands. Big hands, with long, blunt fingers, scarred and callused. Not pretty by a long stretch. Certainly nothing for her to be fantasizing about.

Unaware of the tumult in her head, Tye was thoroughly exploring every inch of his son. He counted fingers and toes, ran his palm over the smooth baby skin and traced a small, brown birthmark on Ryan's abdomen. When he glanced up at her, his expression was exuberant.

"I have one exactly like this!" he told her.

She knew. She'd been trying to forget it since the day Ryan had been born, but now more than ever, the memories crowded in, demanding to be recognized.

Tye was still holding her gaze with his and she could see the change in his face as he realized what she was thinking—she'd traced that very birthmark with her mouth.

In his eyes, a molten gold awareness flared. "We've never talked about what happened that night," he reminded her in a deep, soft tone.

"There's nothing to talk about," she snapped, knowing he could hear the desperation in her voice.

Tye laughed, and Ryan startled at the unfamiliar sound. Tye lifted the baby into his arms and lowered his cheek to brush over the soft, dark down of his son's head. "That's not how I remember it," he said, still chuckling.

Her face felt beet red; she couldn't think of a single intelligent syllable to utter in response. Dulcie almost snatched Ryan from Tye's arms, moving toward the door and waiting for him to leave. "I have to feed him now," she said.

Tye nodded. "By all means." He walked through the door, then turned and gave her one last, satisfied smile before sauntering down the hallway. "While you're feeding him, why don't you search for those lost memories?"

She watched him go, half of her wanting to throw something at him and the other half wanting to run her hands over those shoulders and see if they really felt as firm and slick as she thought they had That Night.

* * *

He should have been thrilled that he was finished helping Uncle Ike, Tye thought later that day. How many times while he was repairing fences, unclogging water holes or riding after a straggling calf in a cloud of dust had he longed for his freedom and a good camera?

It was time to get some more assignments lined up. For over a decade, photographing what magazines called "the Western way of life" had been his love and his life; for the last half of that time, he'd had assignments booked as far in advance as a year from one publication or another.

So why wasn't he as excited about the thought of a new photographic challenge as he used to be? The answer was simple, he figured. Until things were settled between Dulcie and him, he was bound to have some concern about leaving the ranch. But that was temporary. They would marry and work everything out, if he had to tie her to a post to do it, and then he'd get back into the swing of things.

Having such a flexible schedule had been a real blessing—he didn't know another soul who could afford the time or the financial loss to take almost a year off to help out a relative. Of course he would have quit any job he'd had to go when Ike Bradshaw had needed him. He owed his uncle. Taking over the ranch until Ike's leg healed was only a small way to repay him for the home and the love he'd offered Tye.

Still, his flexible schedule was a bit of a curse, too. Time was passing, passing him by. If he didn't get something out there soon, he'd be sacrificing the name he'd spent the past ten years making for himself. It wasn't the money angle, he knew. He could work a hell of a lot less and still make a modest living, which was all anyone could ask. No, it was the seductive lure of acclaim. He *liked* the recognition he got with his photographs. And having people out there actually collecting them was the icing on the cake.

Tye definitely had to get back to work.

He saw little of Dulcie that morning. She seemed to divide her time between Ryan, the kitchen and the other endless chores a ranch generated for everyone who lived there. He felt strangely out of place with nothing to do.

She accepted his offer to play with Ryan during one of his waking periods, and while he was doing so, he realized he was itching for a camera. Surely he could catch that fretful little pucker Ryan's mouth made when Tye disappeared from his line of vision. And how would that frenetic, restless newborn energy translate into a still photo? While he was contemplating angles and light and lenses, Ryan got sleepy and Dulcie whisked him off for a nap.

She was extraordinarily careful to treat him as politely as she would a guest she didn't know well, and he had the strongest urge to shake her, to get right in her face and force her to acknowledge him. *Remember me? I'm the guy you made love with the day your marriage ended. You know, the father of your baby? The one who wants to marry you?*

Instead, he called his agent when she left the room with Ryan. McNally was delighted to hear from Tye, and he promised to get right on a few calls to see who might be interested.

As Tye hung up the receiver, a loud gong rang outside. It probably was nothing more than a signal to the hands that lunch was served, but it was only a little past eleven. The hair rose instinctively on the back of his neck, and he strode toward the back door. He'd heard similar bells before, and at odd times of the day like this they often meant there was trouble.

At the back door, he had to stand aside for Angel and Dulcie, who all but shoved him out of the way in their haste. As the three of them spilled out of the house, a cowboy kneeling in the bed of a pickup nearby waved his hat and hollered.

"Miss Angel, the boss done got himself flattened under his horse."

Angel's face paled and Dulcie gasped in horror. Tye felt sick inside. A man was no match for a half ton of horseflesh. If Day had gone down beneath the full weight of the animal, he might not be in very good shape.

"Is he conscious?" Tye shouted.

The hand looked over the women's heads, clearly surprised by the strange voice. But apparently the authority in Tye's voice rang true, because the man barely hesitated.

"Yup."

Angel scrambled up over the tailgate of the pickup. Dulcie, somewhat shorter and only three weeks out of childbirth, was a little slower. Tye set his hands at her waist and boosted her up, then leaped up behind her, swearing as his weight bore down on his injured finger for an instant.

Day lay in the truck bed, wincing in pain. His right leg was wrapped in a makeshift bandage torn from someone's saddle blanket; blood had soaked through it.

Angel knelt beside him, but Tye noticed it was Dulcie who immediately began a medical assessment, checking her brother's pupils and pulse before beginning to loosen the bandage.

"Get me the med kit!" she shouted at one of the gathered cowboys, and instantly a man broke away and ran toward the barn.

"What'd you do?" she asked her brother.

"Bandolier almost stepped on a snake," Day grunted. "I was thinking about something else, and I came clear out of my seat. Damned horse came down half on me and then stepped square on my leg getting back on his feet." He looked mildly ashamed at the admission, and indeed, a current of amusement was audible among the cowhands as they realized their boss wasn't fatally injured.

Dulcie began probing the wound.

"Hey!" Day yelped in surprise.

"Don't be a baby," Dulcie said. "You're going to live."

"Well, that's a relief," Day replied. He gave his wife a crooked grin and reached up with his good hand to wipe away a tear that was straggling down Angel's cheek. "I'm okay," he said to her quietly, pulling her face into his shoulder.

Dulcie had unwrapped the bandage and was applying pressure to a long, ragged gash, while her other hand investigated the surrounding tissue for additional damage. "This could be broken," she pronounced. "And it's too messy for me to splint. Besides, you need a lot of stitches and—" she held up her finger when her brother would have interrupted "—from the way your face scrunches up when you breathe, I'd say you probably have a couple of ribs broken. Off to the hospital you go, big bro."

Tye considered it a measure of the real pain Day must have been feeling that he didn't protest. "I can drive if you direct me," he said to Dulcie.

Day shot him an unreadable glance. "You feel well enough?"

"Fine," Tye responded evenly.

Day nodded. Then, showing his true nature, he began to issue orders. "Angel, go get Ryan for Dulcie. He'll have to come along. Wes, can you take over here and keep an eye on Beth Ann until Angel gets home?"

A grizzled older man stepped forward and nodded. "I already sent Smoky out with two others to see what he could do for Bandolier." He paused, then took off his hat and beat it against his leg. "We'll try, boss, but it looked to me like that leg snapped."

Day stilled, his hand convulsively clenching into a fist. "Damn. He was the best cutter I ever had." He turned his eyes to the cloudless sky, shutting them all out for a moment.

Dulcie seized the opportunity to slide off the back of the pickup and motion Tye to join her. "I'm going to ride back here with him. Angel can help with Ryan and direct you to the hospital—if you can't find your way back." She gave him a teasing smile, but before he could react, her face sobered. "Go easy but get us there as fast as you can. I'm afraid there might be internal damage."

Angel came rushing out of the house with Ryan then. Dulcie swiftly secured him in the infant seat one of the hands had strapped into the truck, and before Tye could say another word to her, he found himself driving out the ranch road, trying to avoid the worst of the ruts.

Four

The emergency room was deathly quiet. Apparently there weren't many other people in unexpected peril today.

Ryan was awake and starting to squeak, but Dulcie was too uptight to register her son's fussiness. Day's face had been the color of paper by the time they'd arrived at the hospital. It was entirely possible he was just in shock, but she was terribly worried that he'd suffered more serious injuries than she'd been able to assess with her limited medical skill.

Across the waiting room, Tye caught her eye. "Want me to change Ryan?"

"No, thank you." She felt her face growing warm as she laid the baby down. Tye was going to think she was a terrible mother, ignoring her own child like this.

She felt him watching her—probably waiting for her to make a mistake. When she was finished, Tye spoke again.

"I'll be glad to hold him if you need a break."

No! But she nodded, aware that her reaction was irrational.

It was evident from the easy way Tye handled the baby that he'd been around children. It was a disquieting feeling, knowing that she was no longer the only parent in Ryan's life who could take care of him. They'd shared a stiff, uneasy silence ever since Angel had disappeared through the emergency room doors with Day's stretcher. She knew she should thank Tye for his help, but the truth was, she still wasn't sure she even wanted him to be there.

This situation, this moment in time, was a family matter. Memories would be made today and talked of in years to come by those who called the Red Arrow home. Now Tye was a part of those memories whether she liked it or not.

A hand on her shoulder jerked her out of her thoughts. Tye stood behind her, holding the diaper bag in one hand and a flailing, crying Ryan against his shoulder with the other.

"He's hungry," Tye said. "He's been sucking on my finger for the last few minutes but he's getting too smart to be satisfied with that."

The last thing she wanted was to have to sit here and nurse Ryan under Tye's watchful eyes, but she guessed she didn't have a choice. Tye didn't look like he was in the mood to respect a request for privacy.

Settling in a corner, she made do with a blanket over her shoulder.

Tye made no effort to pretend he wasn't interested; every time her gaze collided with his, he watched her with an odd speculation in his amber eyes. By the twentieth time it happened, she was sick and tired of pretending to ignore him.

After she finished feeding Ryan and laid him in the crook of her arm again, she was ready for a good fight. "Do you always stare at women this way or have I been singled out for some special reason?"

"You've been singled out."

"Oh, goody."

"Don't be a wiseacre. It doesn't become you," Tye told her mildly.

"I don't particularly care what becomes me," she said, her voice forceful, though she was careful not to raise her volume and disturb the baby dozing on her shoulder. "I want to know what you're thinking."

"Right now?"

"Right now."

He grinned. "I was thinking that you look awful cute when you're mad. I was thinking that you look pretty fantastic for a woman who just had a baby three weeks ago, and that—"

"Stop it!" She knew her face was burning. Her mind raced, but no brilliant retort came forth. By the time she quit thinking about what to say, too much time had passed.

Tye was grinning broadly. For the first time since he'd seen Ryan and she'd refused his offer of marriage, she didn't sense the taut aura of anger surrounding him.

The swinging door from the treatment area banged open and Angel walked out. Instantly, Dulcie was on her feet. Tye was right behind her. "What's up?" she asked.

Angel offered them both a strained smile. "He's all right," she reassured Dulcie. "Nineteen stitches in the leg and a fractured rib, but nothing more serious."

Thank heavens. She hadn't realized how tense she was until she felt the knot in her stomach ease. Day was the only brother she had, terrible tease and staunch protector all in one. He was her earliest memory and her dearest friend. "So we can take him home?"

Angel's smile faded and she shook her head. "Not today. The doctor wants him on intravenous antibiotics for twenty-four hours to ward off infection. Good old Bandolier really hacked up his leg and ground in the dirt for good measure."

Dulcie sighed, knowing how all cowboys reacted to the thought of a night in the hospital. "He'll be impossible."

Angel's expression was droll. "He already is. Want to talk to him?"

Day was in a private room on the second floor. As they rode up in the elevator, Dulcie was aware that Tye hadn't asked her if he should accompany her. He'd simply picked up the diaper bag and followed as if he'd been invited.

She barely made it through the door of Day's room before her brother began to fire orders at her.

"Whoa," she said. "Don't I even get to kiss the invalid and see the wounds?"

"No." Day didn't even pause. "Of all the damned dumb luck ... We're already shorthanded since Mosey took off. I don't have time for this."

Mosey was a cowhand who had quit suddenly a week earlier. Pretty lousy timing, Dulcie knew, just about the time the cows started dropping calves. Spring was a busy time on a cow-calf operation.

"I could help out."

The quiet statement stopped Day in midsentence. "You?" His eyes narrowed and Dulcie held her breath, but it appeared his accident had knocked some sense into her brother because he didn't say anything else.

"Yup." All of a sudden, Tye had become a man of few words, also.

"Feelin' up to it?"

It was an innocent enough question on the surface, but Dulcie could almost see Tye bristle. Insinuating that something as trivial as an injured hand or a concussion could keep him out of the saddle apparently irked him as much as it had Day.

"I'm feelin' fine," Tye said, clipping the words so short that she wouldn't have been surprised if he'd bitten his tongue.

"You worked on your family's operation, you said."

"My uncle's."

Why did Tye find it necessary to explain that it was his uncle's ranch, she wondered.

"What'd ya do?"

"I was his foreman for ten months."

"Would you be willing to do that for me? For a fee, of course." Her brother's eyes were intent as he regarded Tye. She was absurdly proud that Tye didn't seem intimidated, then chastised herself for caring.

Tye nodded slowly. "I could help out for a few weeks."

Day snorted. "I'm not going to be out of the saddle that long. Now come over here and let me tell you what needs doin.'"

Dulcie, suddenly ignored, looked back at Angel, who only shrugged and smiled. "Let's go get a drink," she whispered.

Dulcie took Ryan from Tye and followed Angel down the hall to the lounge. They got sodas from a machine and sat. Ryan slept peacefully in his knapsack anchored against her chest. Neither woman spoke.

Finally, Angel broke the silence. "So Tye is Ryan's father."

Slowly, Dulcie nodded.

"I had a feeling yesterday that he wasn't just a casual acquaintance." Angel's smile was smug.

"We weren't—" How to explain this? Angel had been her friend since childhood, but there was no easy way to tell this story. "We met while I was still married, and while Lyle was traveling we went to the movies and out for dinner a few times, but it was just a friendship then. He was tired of women who wanted instant relationships and I...I guess I was just lonely."

"We knew things were rough for you," Angel said.

"I didn't cheat on Lyle." Why did she feel the need to make that clear? She was a grown woman. But Day had been more than just a brother throughout most of her life; it was important to her that he and Angel understood. "Nothing happened between us until the day I went back to Albuquerque that last time." She laughed, as a sad memory surfaced of the naive girl she'd been. "Actually, I went back because I'd talked with Lyle on the phone and I thought maybe we had a chance of saving our marriage. I was prepared to forget about the divorce papers."

"What changed your mind?" Angel asked when silence fell again.

"I found Lyle in bed with another woman." She winced. "Well, actually, they were on the kitchen table. And when I left, Tye happened to be in the hallway."

"Oh." Angel's eyes had rounded. "I see. Marriage to Lyle was no picnic for you to start with. He was a real jerk." Her quiet voice expressed a venom all the more remarkable coming from such a tolerant woman.

"Yep." She'd fought and conquered those feelings in the past year. She'd even been genuinely sorry when he'd been killed, mostly because she was happy. She was home, on the ranch where she belonged, and she was going to have a baby of her very own.

"So what happens now?" Angel looked concerned. "Is Tye going to want joint custody of Ryan?"

"I don't know." She met her sister-in-law's troubled gaze. "He asked me to marry him, but I said no. He is not a happy camper right now."

Angel's eyes grew even bigger and a soft, wry smile curved her mouth. "I guess he isn't." She shook her head, and when she looked at Dulcie again her eyes held amusement. "He oozes sex appeal—are you going to be able to resist him?"

"He oozes sex appeal?" Dulcie laughed aloud at the phrase. "I thought you were madly in lust with my brother. Besides, you're married."

"Putting on this gold band doesn't mean I lost my eyesight," Angel said mildly. "And you didn't answer the question."

Dulcie shrugged. "Tye's used to getting what he wants, but I'm not available. Besides, his job is just like Lyle's, and I'll never, ever marry a man who isn't going to stay in one place for the rest of his life. Actually, I doubt I'll ever marry again."

Angel rolled her eyes. "You're awfully young to be making that kind of prediction. I hope you like to eat your words." She smiled. "So Tye is a salesman?"

Dulcie shook her head. "He's an artist. He takes pictures."

"Pictures of what?"

It was too hard to explain. Instead, she dug into the diaper bag, where she'd stashed the magazine Tye had pointed out the night before. It wasn't that she was going to read it—she just had thought it might be good to have it handy in case she had time to kill at a doctor's office or something.

Handing Angel the magazine, she pointed to the cover photo. "He took that."

"You're kidding."

The awe in Angel's voice would have been gratifying if she cared for Tye—which of course, she didn't. Not romantically, anyway. He'd been what she needed at a time when her life was in ruins around her—that was all.

Angel spoke again. "Duls, there's taking pictures and then there's *taking pictures*. This is professional work."

"I hope so. That's all he does."

Angel laughed. "Well, at least one of my fears has been laid to rest. Tye can't be hurting for money if he's making the cover of magazines like this."

Angel knew what she was talking about, Dulcie was sure. She'd been a popular actress before she'd married Day, and the ins and outs of entertainment of all sorts were as familiar to her as birthing calves was to Dulcie. Still, the money was beside the point, even if he was able to make a good living as a photographer. Money didn't make people happy.

Angel was standing, the magazine still in her hand. "May I show this to Day?"

Dulcie shrugged as they walked back to her brother's hospital room. "I guess so."

The hands had made their own evening meal, and she presumed Tye had done the same. Sitting in the family room giving Ryan his evening feeding, Dulcie was very aware of the quiet surrounding her.

Albuquerque hadn't been a particularly noisy city. Though it lacked the genteel bustle of Santa Fe, she thought she preferred its no-nonsense hum of activity. But the bottom line was that she wasn't a city gal at heart. The peaceful silence of the range suited her best.

She closed her eyes and laid her head against the back of the sofa. Ryan was almost asleep at her breast, and she smiled to herself as she felt the tugging of his tiny mouth lessen, his infant body relaxing. Yes, this was where she belonged. She and her son. She would teach him to love the ranch as much as she did.

"Is he sleeping?"

Tye's hushed voice jolted her. She'd assumed he was already in his room for the evening. As she stiffened reflexively, Ryan began to nurse vigorously for an instant. Quickly, she scrambled to cover her exposed flesh with a baby blanket, but Tye caught a corner of it, stopping her.

"Please—may I watch him?" His gaze wasn't directed at her, but at his son's tiny body. He reached out, and she suppressed a gasp, sure he was going to place his hand right on her naked flesh, but he stopped short, passing a gentle finger over the shape of Ryan's perfect oval skull. "He's a miracle," he whispered.

She felt her face growing hot as she struggled with her feelings, looking away. Tye had already seen her before; it wasn't as if she needed to be modest. And he was far more interested in Ryan than he was in her—that was for sure.

"Dulcie—" Tye's hand moved to cup her chin, drawing her head up. "Don't be embarrassed. This is a beautiful sight to me. I'm glad you decided to breast-feed our son." He carefully smoothed one tiny foot between his thumb and forefinger. "It must be a pretty fantastic feeling to know that you can provide everything he needs to grow strong and healthy right now."

The intensity of his quiet words and the warm light in his eyes stole every molecule of oxygen right out of the air around her. It would be so easy to give in to that warmth.

She liked the intimacy of the three of them—father, mother, child. And Tye made her feel cherished, special, with the reverent way he treated her, as if bearing a child wasn't an everyday occurrence but truly the miracle he saw.

Maybe she liked the intimacy too much. It made her long for permanence, for a commitment that meant more to Tye than financial support and an occasional stopover between jobs. And that was something she couldn't have.

She'd best not forget it, either.

Carefully, she slipped a finger into the side of Ryan's tiny rosebud mouth, breaking the suction. His head lolled back against her arm as she covered her breast and propped him upright.

"Time for a bubble," she said, rubbing the baby's back and studiously ignoring Tye. In seconds, a hefty burp rolled up from the depths of the baby's stomach. Ryan didn't wake up, and she smiled faintly as she looked over his head at Tye. "Would you like to take him up to bed?"

Tye's expression told her that he knew she'd withdrawn from him deliberately. But he said nothing, merely took the baby from her and moved toward the stairs. She watched them go, father cradling son against his heart, and her own heart ached. She hadn't been woman enough to hold one man, and she wasn't fool enough to try it again...no matter how much she was tempted.

Adjusting her clothing, she turned off the lights downstairs and refilled the glass of ice water that was a nursing mother's constant companion. Then she mounted the steps and moved down the hall toward her own room, conscious of how very tired she was. The day had been draining.

The door to her room was ajar. As she moved into the dark interior, she put out a hand to flip the switch on the wall, but before she could find it, a large body steamrolled into her.

"Wha...?"

"Holy thunderin' tarnation! What in hell is that?"

Even before she reached over and found the light switch, she knew she'd slopped water from the glass she held. Apparently, Tye was wearing it now.

The room filled with light. Tye stood before her, pulling at his soaking shirt with thumb and forefinger. He glared at her. "Since when do you carry around ice water in the dark?"

"Since I started breast-feeding your son," she replied sternly. "Since when do you start sneaking around in my room?"

His eyes narrowed, but instead of flinging another dart at her, he pointed to her bedside table. "I didn't know what to do with Ryan's pacifier, and I wanted you to be able to find it fast," he said.

Her gaze followed his finger's direction. There was the pacifier. And really, she'd known he must have had a reason. Tye had been nothing but chivalrous in the time they'd spent together. She exhaled slowly. "I'm sorry," she said, forcing herself to look at him squarely. "I'm tired and I overreacted. Thank you."

She stepped aside, waiting for him to leave.

But Tye didn't move.

Then he took a step toward her. One large hand lifted, reached out and snagged hers, drawing her closer. At the same time, the look in his eyes warmed with humor. "What am I going to do about my shirt?"

She swallowed. Just because he was the most compelling, magnetic hunk of male that she'd ever met in her entire life didn't mean that she had to act like a simpleton. She cleared her throat, waiting for a witty retort to spring to mind. "I . . . I don't know."

"Guess you'll have to warm me up." Slowly he pulled her to him, running his palms up and down her back, flattening her body against his beneath the soaked garment.

She gasped at the clammy cold that seeped through her shirt instantly. Within a moment, though, the sodden fabric was forgotten when Tye dropped his head and his mouth nuzzled along her cheek. "Meet me halfway, Duls," he whispered.

She might have resisted his overpowering sex appeal. She might even have resisted that glint of humor lurking in the depths of his eyes. But the entreaty in his voice, the uncertainty that broke through, erased any thought of refusal. *He needed her.* In what way, for how long, became unimportant. Her body relaxed into his in tacit acceptance.

Releasing the restraint on her common sense was her undoing. His breath was a hot lick of sensation against the sensitive lobe of her ear, and a shiver started at the top of her spine, racing steadily down to center in the feminine heart of her. Her muscles loosened, her knees felt weak. At her back, the large hands that held her firmly against him slipped down to cup and fondle her buttocks. He bent his knees slightly, and in the same moment, tightened his grip on her bottom. She cried out, in both shock and arousal, as she suddenly found herself riding his thigh, the hot, wanting pulse at the top of her legs pressed flush against the hard ridge of male power contained by his jeans.

Tye groaned. She turned her face into his neck as her arms stole up around his wide shoulders. She pressed reckless kisses against the strong column of his throat as he slowly shifted her over him. Beneath her palms, the strong muscles of his back flexed; he pulled back just far enough to dip his head and capture her mouth with his.

Chain lightning. Liquid heat. His lips were soft and silky, but the rough man-flesh of his jaw scraped her as he angled his mouth over hers. His tongue plunged deep, with no thought of the months that stood between them. She responded as she had the last time he'd kissed her, accepting his tongue and sucking lightly, curling her own tongue around his in welcome.

Feverishly, she twisted in his arms, her body sliding over his, her mouth giving him everything he demanded. *She had missed this.* Oh, God, she had missed this, missed Tye.

The thought was as cold as the ice water that had slopped down his shirt. What was she thinking? Missing Tye meant that she was incomplete without him. Missing Tye meant that he could hurt her when he left, as she knew he would. Lyle hadn't stayed for her. Tye wouldn't, either.

And she refused to let it matter.

Tearing her mouth from his, she pressed against his chest until he raised his head. She could see puzzlement rising in his eyes as he let her slide to the floor.

"Wait—I can't just do this. I have to think."

"Don't think." He molded her bottom in his big hands and rubbed himself roughly against her again. "Just feel."

She shuddered, closing her eyes against the appeal in his blunt features. "I'm not looking for a man."

His hands clenched briefly on her bottom, but for a long moment he was silent. She opened her eyes. His expression had darkened, passion replaced by anger.

"Like it or not, you already have a man. If you didn't want a man in your life, you should have thought a little bit before you hopped into my bed and got pregnant with my son."

She sucked in a shocked breath, cut to the core by his accurate words. There was no defense, and she knew it as well as he did. She had made it impossible for him to resist her that night.

Tye grabbed her chin and pulled her face up to his, taking her mouth in a hard, bruising kiss that conveyed contempt. Then he pushed her away from him and stalked out of her room.

If he could manage it, he would kick himself around the barn and back, Tye thought as he rinsed his cereal bowl the next morning. He knew what Dulcie's life had been like. He knew how gently she needed to be handled, and yet what had he done? Fondled her against her will—never mind that she had eventually responded, he knew it wasn't what she had wanted. And then, when he should have apologized and backed off, he'd accused her of jumping his bones and practically told her that this whole sorry mess was her fault.

He blew out a deep breath, shaking his head. He had no one to blame but himself for missing Dulcie's pregnancy and Ryan's birth. He'd been aware from the first moment he'd parted her legs and sunk into her body that night that he wasn't protected. He'd known a baby was more than a remote possibility, and yet he'd let almost a year slip by.

The telephone rang. Startled out of his thoughts, he grabbed for it as he glanced at his watch. It wasn't even seven in the morning. Who could be calling so early? "Red Arrow Ranch."

"Tye? 'Zat you, you ornery sidewinder?"

"McNally." Hell, he thought. He never should have told Bill McNally where he was going to be. The last person he wanted to talk to right now was his agent. Bill had been itching to load him up with assignments for months; he probably had a dozen jobs lined up.

"Hey, buddy. So your ranchin' days are finally over. I thought I'd never pry you outta Montana! Whatcha doin' 'way down there? Find somethin' to take pictures of?"

"No, I came down to visit a friend," Tye responded. "I know you didn't call just to hear the sound of my voice. What have you got?"

"Well..." Bill's voice was sly. "How soon do you want to start?"

He thought quickly. "I'm helping out a friend down here. It'll be at least three weeks. You'd better give me a month."

"A month?" It was a disgruntled squeak. "Hell, you could have gotten five jobs under your belt by then."

"Maybe so, but it'll be that long before I'm free. Can you work something up for me then?"

"Um-hm, let's see...rodeo, Dallas. Branding, Rockin' M. Parimutuel, Albuquerque Downs, then up to Oregon for a new huntin' lodge. And you got a gallery showing in Santa Fe you really oughta show for, buddy. Some of your biggest buyers are coming to town, and you know how they like to meet the guy who took the pictures.''

Tye sighed. ''Okay. That all sounds fine. Just get me the itinerary, and I'll take care of transportation.''

Bill was silent for a minute. ''You don't seem too thrilled 'bout all this. You got a problem I don't know about?''

''Nah.'' He wasn't ready to share Dulcie and Ryan with anyone yet. ''I guess being in one place for so long made me start to like it.''

''Can't 'zactly blame you for that, buddy. You been doin' this routine for a lotta years now.''

Tye was mildly astonished, and his voice showed it. ''Am I talking to Bill-the-Money-Maker McNally? Is this the same man who's hounded me to death to stay out there and make a name for myself for over a dozen years?''

A chuckle drifted out of the receiver. ''Had to whip you into shape, didn't I? And I did,'' he added with a touch of pride. ''But I been around enough artsy temperaments now to know that if you ain't happy, your work's gonna show it. You think you need a change, you just call old Bill and we'll make us a new plan, you hear?''

''I hear.'' Tye hesitated. ''I'm not unhappy, Bill. I just . . . have a lot on my mind right now.''

''Just as long as it ain't a woman.'' Bill chuckled again. ''I've seen more good men ruined by women than I can count. As long as it ain't woman trouble, you'll come through fine.''

Tye was silent.

On the other end of the line, Bill heaved a huge sigh. "Hell. It *is* a woman, ain't it? Buddy, you better be careful. I ain't got time to be doctoring your broken heart, you hear?"

"I hear." Even to himself, he sounded wimpy. The thought was enough to make a man puke. He straightened from the counter on which he'd been leaning. "Don't worry, Bill, I can take care of myself."

"I'm countin' on it, buddy. I'll get this schedule down to you today, okay?"

"Sounds fine. Be talking to you."

Tye set down the receiver thoughtfully. No doubt about it, he definitely didn't feel the old enthusiasm for his work. Why? He still loved taking photographs, searching out that perfect play of light and shadow, rushing to capture the gritty reality of a workday on a ranch, capturing weariness, eagerness, the death and life that were still the realities of the modern West.

He hadn't felt this way in Montana, this desire to stay planted in one spot. In Montana, he'd had only one desire: to get back to Albuquerque and find Dulcie. Now that he had, he wasn't ready to leave.

As he hustled out to the barn to begin the day's work according to Dulcie's brother's instructions, he forced himself to squarely face that truth: he wasn't ready to leave Dulcie and his son.

He worked with the cowhands all day. Used to the routine, the men chuckled at some of the orders he passed on from their boss as they efficiently accomplished their chores.

It felt good to be in the saddle again. He hadn't realized just how good it would feel until he dismounted from the gelding that evening and felt the wonderful stiffness in his legs that told him he'd been out of the saddle too long. His damaged finger was throbbing, but it was a good ache, and he looked forward to tomorrow's work.

For the next three days, his routine was unchanged. He rode out with Day's men in the morning, relayed orders and didn't come in again until dinnertime. While Dulcie and Angel cleaned up after the meal, he held Ryan and played with him while he gave Day a rundown of the work. By the time they were finished, the women were done in the kitchen, and after Beth Ann went to bed, the adults sat down to watch a television program.

Dulcie was always the first one to head for bed, right around the time Ryan needed another feeding, so he hadn't gotten to exchange a single word with her in private for several days. He was conscious of time slipping by. In three weeks he had to leave again.

It ate away at him relentlessly. Ryan would grow two feet in his absence. Already he was starting to wriggle his little body all over when Tye came in and talked to him. Did he recognize his daddy? Was there some biological homing device that clued in his son or was it just the unfamiliar voice and presence? Ryan didn't do it for Day, he noticed with a certain amount of gratification. Only for his daddy.

Of course, Ryan's mother didn't wriggle for Day, either. The thought made him grin as he came in and washed up on the fourth night of his temporary job.

Five

If anybody lit a match, the room would go up in flames faster than dry prairie grass, Tye thought later that evening. Angel had announced that she wasn't feeling well immediately after dinner and had gone up to her room. Day had followed her less than half an hour later, leaving Dulcie alone with Tye in the living room, if he didn't count Ryan's presence.

It had taken him about three seconds to sense her discomfort.

When he moved to settle his feet on a hassock, she jumped.

He cleared his throat, and her head whipped around toward him so fast that he bet she'd wrenched her neck. Ryan, probably sensing the tension, began to fuss, and she sprang to her feet, pacing the room with him and patting his back.

Given what had happened the last time he'd kissed her, Tye figured she was right to be a little nervous after this most recent episode. Trying to get her to relax, he cast about for a topic of conversation. His gaze lit on photos of Day and Dulcie during their childhood.

"I wonder if Ryan'll look like that when he gets a little older." He gestured to a photo of Dulcie as a fat, drooling baby, a wide grin showing her toothless gums.

She turned at the sound of his voice. Looking back and forth between the picture and her son, she smiled tenderly. "He really doesn't look much like me. I bet if we compared him to your baby pictures, we'd see a big resemblance."

"Then he oughta grow up to be a fine-lookin' man."

She laughed. "And modest, just like his daddy."

She was relaxing by the minute. To keep the conversation going, he said, "And his uncle. I take notice of how modest your brother is, too."

That really got her going. She chuckled. "Day doesn't have a modest bone in his body." The smile softened to a tender expression around the edges. "But I couldn't ask for a better brother. He's always been there when I needed him."

Tye nodded, deliberately rubbing his palm against the side of the jaw Day had punched. "So I've noticed."

She got his meaning. "He does overdo the protectiveness once in a while. But I really can't blame him. He thinks of himself as more of a father than a brother to me."

She had never shared much about her home with him, even when they were in Albuquerque, going out as friends. "Why is that? I know there are a few years between you, but it's not like he's a totally different generation."

"It wasn't that. He's only six years older. But both our parents died before I was out of school. After that, Day raised me."

He knew what it was like to grow up without parents. It marked a person, made 'em different from all the other kids in a way only somebody who'd been through it could understand. "That's tough. I guess you don't have such great memories of your childhood."

She looked at him oddly. "Well, losing Mama and Daddy was rough, but I was fortunate in so many ways. I wasn't uprooted from home, and Day was determined to do everything just like they had.... It could have been worse."

He nodded, wanting her to continue.

"The ranch means so much to me. I never realized until I moved away how badly I would miss it."

"You talked about it constantly in Albuquerque."

She nodded. "When Lyle and I separated, I couldn't wait to come home. And afterward—" she blushed a little and he knew she was remembering what had happened between them "—I knew I needed to come home. Back to the ranch.''

"You seem very happy here.''

"I am." She looked at him squarely. "I belong here. And I don't plan to leave again. Ever.''

He sensed she was spoiling for a fight, and he knew exactly what was the matter. In her eyes, he had a lousy track record when it came to staying in one place, just like her husband. But he wasn't in the mood for an argument, so he ignored her aggressive words and instead said, "Ranching suits you. You don't hesitate to get your hands dirty if you're needed.''

Her sober mood seemed to lighten again. Against her shoulder, Ryan had ceased his fussing and his little head lolled in slumber. "When I was born, my daddy bought me a brand of my very own, along with a heifer. Every year since then, I've gotten a heifer for my birthday. Every other calf out of my heifers gets my brand. Day keeps a separate record of them—I think there are close to a hundred head now.''

She gently patted the back of the baby in her arms. "I'm going to get him a brand and do the same. That way, when he's grown, he'll have a head start on a herd of his own. When he's older, he'll have to learn to ride and rope, to pull calves and give shots and brand his animals. I learned it all firsthand," she went on, and he could hear the pride in her voice, "And although I don't spend much time out now that I'm needed in the house, I could do it if I had to.''

"I guess you were a dedicated 4-H'er in your day.''

"You betcha." She pointed to an album resting on a shelf below the photos, and her voice took on a self-conscious tone. "That's my scrapbook with the ribbons sticking out of the top. Too bad those blue ribbons didn't translate into skills that would help me as an adult."

Now her voice sounded defeated, just like she'd sounded when he'd first met her. She'd been alone then, stuck in a city apartment while her husband trotted off without her. Now she was here, in the bosom of her family, with a child at her breast and a herd of her own, and she was still alone. He wondered if she knew it.

He stood, and she immediately backed up a step. "I, uh, should go and put Ryan down."

"May I say good-night to him?" His question stopped her in the act of rushing from the room.

She half turned, so the baby's soft features and slack little mouth were facing him. "If you like."

He walked toward her. When he was close enough to touch, he stopped, sliding one of his fingers beneath Ryan's far tinier ones. "Sweet dreams, cowboy," he said, bending to touch his lips to his son's forehead. "See you in the morning." He lifted his head and looked at Dulcie, a heartbeat away over the sleeping child. "It's early. Will you come back down for a while?"

She hesitated.

"We need to have some time to talk," he pressed.

"All right." It was a quiet agreement to his demand as she turned away. "Let me settle him."

While she was gone, he wandered over to the bookshelf to get a better look at the photographs. Her childhood scrapbook drew him like a magnet, and he slowly slipped it from the shelf, feeling as if he was prying, though he told himself she wouldn't have pointed it out to him if she minded him looking at it.

She'd been loved—that much was obvious. Even if her parents hadn't lived to see her grown, they'd loved her. The pictures were evidence of that. When she was a gap-toothed grade-schooler, the photos with her parents in them stopped abruptly. For a year or two, so did her smiles.

But gradually, he could see the healing, and by the time she was a teenager she was glowing with good health and adolescent beauty. Interspersed with the photos were blue ribbons, county-fair programs with her entries heavily underlined and grainy newspaper photos yellowed now with age showing Dulcie with champion heifers. The blue ribbons and the many others she'd accumulated were largely for roping and calf raising at first, but as she got older, he was surprised to see an equal number of first-place wins in food entries for preserves and pies.

The next few pages were devoted to high school graduation and then her wedding. She looked happy, he thought. Apparently she hadn't had any concerns about her husband-to-be at first. He studied the groom. It was only the second time in his life he'd ever seen the guy close up, but he wasn't impressed. Lyle Meadows looked ... soft. Not nearly the kind of man Dulcie needed.

"Seen enough?"

Startled, he slapped the book closed and said the first thing that came into his head. "You got first place for your pecan pie just last summer. And you took second in the canning category."

"Yeah." She took the book from him and replaced it on the shelf. It seemed to him that she fiddled with it a while longer than necessary.

"Well, that's great," he said. Already, she was as uptight as she'd been earlier.

"It's nothing special," she said.

He didn't like hearing her put herself down. "It is special. Superb baking and cooking can be just as much a talent as roping and barrel racing. You must be proud of those ribbons."

She didn't answer. Her sudden lack of confidence brought back a vivid memory of the dispirited woman he'd met in Albuquerque. Apparently, her ex hadn't gone out of his way to shower her with compliments.

As he watched, she pulled another album from the shelf and extended it to him. "You might be interested in this one."

When his eyebrows rose in query, she added, "I've begun keeping a baby book for Ryan."

He reached for the keepsake slowly, fighting the unexpected rush of feelings that ran through him at her words.

Dulcie watched his face as he leafed through the little book. It was obvious that he was fascinated by anything to do with Ryan. His big hands moved across the pictures, tracing the memories she'd recorded for her son. Slowly he scanned the album, and she wondered what he was thinking as he took in the photos Angel had taken in the delivery room of Ryan screaming his head off while the nurses checked him over, on the scales, in his first bath. When he came to the line on which she had recorded his name as Ryan's father, he nodded once, an abrupt motion that he cut off in mid nod.

A thick packet of photos in a folder fell out of the back of the album. Mesmerized by his long, strong fingers and the curling chestnut hairs liberally sprinkled over the backs of his hands, she didn't realize immediately what he was looking at.

"Wait," she said belatedly. "Those aren't of Ryan—" Too late.

Tye already had withdrawn the photos and was staring at the one on the top. In it, she was mucking out a stall in the barn. She had a pitchfork in her hand and a bandanna around her head. She was wearing dirty overalls but the side buttons wouldn't meet. It had been taken when she was about six months pregnant.

As he flipped through the rest of the stack, the tension in the room grew. She could see a muscle ticking in his jaw and she rushed into meaningless chatter to get them past the awkward moment.

"Every time I turned around, Angel was taking pictures of me. I wasn't real thrilled and I promised her that when her turn comes, she can expect a payback. Only trouble is, when her turn comes, Angel won't look like a big ol' heifer past her due date. Tall women always carry babies well. It's the short ones like me that have these huge bellies sticking out in front, clearing the path before us.'' She knew she was running on too much, but the sadness clouding his eyes was making her feel so guilty that she couldn't stand still. His hands hung limp, and she gently took the photos from him, slipping them back into their envelope and replacing them in the back of the album.

"Look, Tye," she said quietly, "I'm as sorry as can be that you weren't here for—and before—Ryan's birth. I guess I was thinking like an ostrich . . . if I just buried my head in the dirt long enough, all the problems would blow over. But what's done is done. I guess now we just have to go on from here."

"Go on?" The words exploded from his lips.

Too late, she realized that anger had replaced regret, and that she was the closest target at hand.

"How in the hell can we go on when you won't marry me?" he snarled. "My son is illegitimate. Nothing you can do or say can change that fact. And the one thing that could is the one thing you won't consider."

He spun on his heel and stalked to the other side of the room, rubbing the back of his neck with one tanned hand. "Maybe you don't think it's a big deal, but I think different. I *know* different."

Her hackles rose and she opened her mouth to blast him. But before she could spit out her thoughts, his words brought back in a rush the things he'd said to her in Day's study the night he'd arrived. He'd shouted at her, told her he knew what it was like to be a kid without a legal father, though he hadn't phrased it so delicately. He'd been so furious he'd been shaking.

He probably hated her for putting him in this position.

She had no right to shout at him. She'd done him a great wrong. Setting aside her own feelings, she chose her words carefully. "From what you said the other night, I gather you didn't know your father at all."

He snorted, an ugly, mirthless sound. "Hell, I don't even know who my father was. And if my mother knew, which is a real big if, she never said. She took off when I was six and we never heard another word from her until somebody sent her belongings home after she died, so I'll never know."

He might be over six feet tall, but all she could see was the hurting little boy who'd wanted desperately to know he was loved. She was overly emotional right now anyway, courtesy of postpregnancy hormones, and she felt tears welling in her eyes as she imagined his childhood. "What a horrible thing to do to a child."

Rather than soothing him, her words had the opposite effect. "Don't waste your pity on me," he said, his eyes blazing. "My uncle raised me. He and my aunt and my cousins were my real family, and even if I'd had both parents, I probably wouldn't have had it so good. They treated me like a son, even indulged my passion for photography from the time I first started foolin' around with a camera."

"Still," she persisted, "I'm sure there were moments when you felt alone, when you felt that you didn't really belong. It would have been only natural."

The silence was so taut she could have snapped it like a strip of rotten rubber. He looked so furious that for a single moment she was afraid she'd overstepped the bounds of his tolerance and unleashed a cougar. *Flee!* urged a small voice in her head, but she squashed it as fast as she acknowledged it. And not only because she trusted Tye to conquer his rage.

She'd always preferred to face her nightmares rather than trying to outrun them. And she knew she couldn't outrun Tye if he chose to hunt her down.

As the last thought flashed through her mind, his expression changed. As quickly as it had built, his inner storm seemed to spend itself and his anger drained away.

Gruffly, he said, "Yeah. I guess it's natural for kids to be curious about their parents."

Anxious now to reassure him, she said, "I hope you know that Ryan will never have any reason to question my love for him."

He looked startled for a moment. "Dulcie, the one thing I don't doubt is your love for our son." He paused. "But have you thought about how Ryan will feel if he ever learns that you refused to give him a father, even when his father was ready and willing to assume the role?"

Oh, he was good. The knife slipped in between her ribs so smoothly that she didn't even feel it until he twisted. Swallowing her own uncertainties, she replied, "Whether or not we marry, Tye, I know you care about Ryan. I have accepted that you are going to be a part of his life. He's going to grow up with the love of two parents."

"But it would be better if we were a family," he pressed.

She shook her head. "Not necessarily. If we can't stick together after the wedding, what's the point?"

Tye grinned, a flash of white teeth against tanned flesh, and her knees suddenly weakened at the sensual knowledge in his gaze. "Duls, the one thing I'm not worried about is how well we stick together."

She blushed. She couldn't help it. His lazy drawl and the memories of just how well they'd "stuck together" played through her mind, sending streamers of excitement through her body, softening and moistening her for the age-old conclusion to this kind of flirtation.

Hurriedly, she said, "That's not what I meant."

The look he slanted in her direction made her shift her body, pressing her knees together to assuage the throbbing between her legs. His gaze narrowed, and she knew he hadn't missed the small motion, but she gathered her common sense and ignored him.

"I was referring to your work."

He looked blank. "What does my work have to do with marrying you?"

Impatience replaced the desire simmering in her blood. "Dammit, Tye, you know as well as I do! I already was married to a man who left me for months on end. I'll never do it again."

"I can't just change my job because the hours don't suit you."

"I'm not asking you to!" She flounced to the other side of the room and threw herself down on the couch. Reaching for the television remote, she punched the buttons with unnecessary force.

The TV came on too loud, and she reduced the volume, then sat gazing with unseeing eyes at the program. Tye came over and sat a few feet from her, but she ignored him. What a mess! Why couldn't he understand how she felt? Why couldn't he just leave her alone? She wasn't going to fight him about seeing Ryan; why couldn't he be satisfied with that?

"I have a showing at a gallery in Santa Fe next month," Tye said quietly. "And I've reserved some time in a darkroom to develop the film I've been shooting. It will take a couple of days."

She couldn't let him see that bothered her—the thought of his leaving. Even if it was only for a few days. That's what Lyle had always said, too. But then she'd get the phone call . . . and the days would stretch into a week, a month and more. Stiffly, she said, "You don't have to explain yourself to me. Save your explanations for Ryan. As he gets older, it will be hard for him to accept his daddy being gone for months at a time."

"It's a few days, Dulcie, not months." Tye's voice was sharp. "I'm not your husband, so why don't you quit punishing me for the things he did?"

That wasn't what she was doing, she wanted to protest. *I'm only trying to protect myself!* The thought was startling. Protect herself from what?

Tye spoke again and his tone had softened. "Besides, I wasn't just trying to explain myself to you. I have something to ask you."

She waited, but he didn't speak until she had turned her head and met his gaze with her own.

"Would you come with me to Santa Fe? I'd like you to be there for my opening so you can get a feel for some of what my work involves."

"I can't—I couldn't possibly leave Ryan." She seized the first thought that came into her head. She didn't want to spend any more time with Tye than she had to. Being able to visualize all the things he did while he was gone would only make it harder, would only make her feel worse when he left for good.

"I didn't expect you to leave Ryan." Tye was oblivious to all the conflicting emotions clamoring for attention within her. "We'll take him along. There's no place that he can't go with us. You can even bring him to the opening." He grinned. "In fact, I insist. I haven't told my agent I have a son. It'll throw him into a total tailspin."

Her breath had caught in her throat at the sudden lightening of his handsome features. His eyes danced and his strong white teeth flashed as he anticipated the moment. She remembered the first time she'd seen him unlocking the door of the neighboring apartment in Albuquerque. Her response had been one of those purely chemical reactions; she'd had to work to keep from drooling when he'd seen her and come across to introduce himself. He'd been perfectly correct when he'd learned that she was married, and she'd felt safe, so safe that she'd even gone for sandwiches with him several times while Lyle was out of town. Purely neighborly outings.

Safe, ha! Her judgment was in serious need of some fine-tuning, obviously. She opened her mouth to tell him she wasn't going to Santa Fe, but he was leaning toward her at the same moment, his gaze on her mouth as he drew closer... and every thought in her head evaporated under the heat of that mouth as he pressed his lips to hers.

"It's settled, then," he said against her mouth. "I'll take care of the reservations."

She couldn't answer. Every brain cell was focused on the sensations of warm, moist heat whispering over her lips, the slick promise of his tongue whisking across her lower lip, the rougher, salty taste of his skin as he raised his head and placed his finger against her still-pursed lips.

"Hold that thought." He was grinning again as he got to his feet. As he ambled across the room and headed for the stairs, she could almost see the satisfaction oozing out of him. The louse.

Then she realized that she was still sitting there, the tips of her fingers lightly touching the lips he had kissed. Why was she calling *him* names?

* * *

She had just put Ryan in his infant seat and turned to start breakfast the next morning when Tye clomped into the kitchen.

"Your brother awake yet?"

"Good morning." She smiled too sweetly to remind him of his omission. "I slept well, thank you for inquiring. And no, I haven't seen Day yet."

Tye smiled, but he looked distracted. "Good morning to you, too. Would you mind going and getting Day?" He walked over to Ryan and easily lifted him into his arms, talking quietly to the baby as she turned and ran up the stairs.

A few minutes later, Day was in the kitchen. He yawned and rubbed a hand over his stubbled jaw, looking significantly at the clock, which didn't even register 6:00 a.m. yet. "What's up?"

"Three of those heifers you looked at last night went into labor a little while ago."

"Three at once? Hell," Day said with disgust. "I thought we still had a good week to wait."

Tye nodded, setting Ryan back in his little carrier. "How're your ribs feelin'?

"Sore. But I guess if I have to pull a calf, they'll just have to get a little sorer."

Tye shook his head. "I can handle it, unless we have two problems at once. Then I'd say we're in trouble."

Neither man stuck around for breakfast. As soon as the rest of the hands had been fed and the dirty dishes cleaned up, Dulcie packed a basket of food and a large thermos of coffee and headed for the barn.

The minute she stepped inside, she could tell something was wrong. Tension hung in the air and settled in the rigid shoulders of the men gathered around a large box stall at the far end of the barn. Two heifers with new calves occupied other stalls as she passed them, but in the third stall, a cow was down.

Her brother balanced on crutches against the rail. Two other hands stood in the doorway of the stall, but she didn't see Tye until she got into the open doorway. Then she saw him, hunkered down in the straw beside the straining heifer. The cow had lost a lot of blood and was clearly exhausted. She lay panting on the straw, too weak even to bellow as labor contractions tightened the girth of her pregnant belly. As they watched, a tiny hoofed leg protruded from the cow's birth canal.

All the men swore in unison. Dulcie silently echoed their feelings. The baby was turned wrong; chances were good that they were going to lose both the heifer and her calf.

Tye was unbuttoning his shirt rapidly as he turned and spoke to Day. "I'm going to have to go in. I called the vet almost two hours ago but we can't wait."

Day nodded grimly, never taking his eyes from the cow as Tye got flat on his belly behind her. The other two hands guarded her legs, ready to rope her if she got a second wind and tried to fight, but even when Tye inserted a hand into the birth canal after a contraction, shoving the tiny limb back inside, she didn't fuss much.

It was a long and messy process. Every time a contraction hit, Tye stopped and waited for it to pass before easing his arm farther inside the cow. She saw him set his teeth against the pain she knew he was feeling, like a giant hand squeezing his arm beyond tolerance. The poor heifer looked as if she was already gone, except for the shallow movement of her flanks and the increasingly weak contractions that rippled through her.

Day kept up a running commentary, firing question after question at Tye as he tried to maneuver the calf into proper position within the birth canal.

"It's a foreleg," Tye reported. "I've got my hand around the skull now but I can't get a grip...."

Finally, just when Dulcie thought they were going to have to admit defeat, Tye gave a grunt of satisfaction. "There! Now if she can just help a little bit, we can get this baby movin'." He changed position, planting his boots against the floor and preparing to pull.

A few minutes later, the calf slipped into the world. While the two other men tried to get the exhausted heifer on its feet, Tye examined the baby. "Nothing looks broken or dislocated," he said with some surprise. "Of course, I can't tell for sure."

Dulcie knew he was hesitant to handle the little calf too much until the mother had accepted it...if the mother lived long enough to do so.

"Go get cleaned up," Day told him. "We'll keep an eye on things here."

Tye nodded. He caught Dulcie's eye as he turned to leave and beckoned her over.

She flew to his side, forgetting for the moment that she would be better off if he wasn't around. "Are you all right?"

Tye flexed his shoulders. "My arm might be bruised, but it can't be any worse than being hit by a truck."

"Looks to me like you've had a lot of practice pulling calves."

He gave her a sidelong look. "I told you I was raised on a ranch. Didn't you believe me?"

She ignored the question, turning on the water and going to a cupboard for a towel. "It's quite a switch from ranching to photography. What got you started?"

He shrugged as the water sluiced over his arm and shoulder. "One of my cousins got a camera for Christmas the year I was ten. She was older than I was, but that camera set in a corner and collected dust until summertime, when I discovered it and asked if I could take a few pictures." He smiled, and she wondered if he knew how pleasant the memories were. "And that was pretty much that. My uncle encouraged me once he saw how interested I was. I got a camera of my own the next Christmas."

"So you realized you enjoyed taking pictures more than rounding up smelly old cows."

Tye's smile faded. "I didn't have much choice. My uncle had two daughters of his own. I didn't expect that I'd have a place at the ranch indefinitely."

She was silent for a minute, wondering about the logic of that. "But obviously you were welcomed when you went home last year."

"My uncle needed someone to direct the troops," he told her. "Both my cousins are married now and their husbands work the ranch, but they aren't the kind of men who could manage the whole operation."

It sounded to her as if Tye had a home and people who cared for and about him, regardless of what he thought. But she sensed that he wasn't willing to listen to that, so she didn't pursue it.

"Did you study photography after you graduated?"

He shook his head. "I took some photography classes in high school, but since then I've been self-taught." He stopped and grinned at her, the charming expression she remembered so well from their early encounters when they had talked casually for hours. "You'll be sorry if you encourage me to talk about my work."

She smiled back. "I doubt that." And it was true. Lyle had never shared anything to do with his work with her. In this respect, at least, Tye was totally different. She had been woolgathering, but gradually she realized that she was still watching Tye. He'd cleaned the blood and dirt from his upper body and was using a towel to blot up the water as he tossed a lock of dark hair back from his forehead.

Her gaze lingered on the curl that fell defiantly over his broad brow, then followed the towel as it whisked across one smooth broad shoulder and down into a circular pattern that buffed both of his flat male nipples into small tight peaks. She recognized and accepted the ribbon of sexual awareness that shivered through her. How could she have forgotten what he looked like? The muscles in his neck were thick and strong, his arms rippled with hard-earned sinew over smooth, golden flesh to which water droplets clung. What she wouldn't give to be one of those drops right now—

The towel dropped to the floor, and she averted guilty eyes from his body. Too late she realized that he was walking across the squeaking floorboards toward her. Hastily, she looked past him at the doorway, measuring the space she would have to cross. But before she could command her body to leave, to escape the hot intent glowing in his gaze, he reached out and clasped her shoulders between his large hands.

"Kiss me," he muttered in a deep, hoarse voice that brooked no refusal.

She would have resisted, she told herself. Of course she would have. But his lips were warm and firm and sure as he plundered her mouth with fierce, bold strokes of his tongue, demanding her response with every silken stroke. His hands slid purposefully down her back to cup her bottom, dragging her up against him until she was barely touching the floor, and she gasped, sliding her arms up around his neck and into his hair, deepening the kiss in helpless submission as the firm thrust of his arousal settled into the sensitive cradle at the apex of her thighs. She was engulfed in an electrical storm of sensation generated by his need.

Why had she ever thought he was civilized? With the exception of venting his justifiable anger about her failure to tell him of her pregnancy, he'd been the soul of decorum and patience. So patient that she'd been lulled into forgetting.

And how could anybody forget this? Her body certainly hadn't. His mere touch ignited an uncontrollable fire within her. Her breasts tingled, begging for his experienced fingers, and she shifted herself against him, creating a pleasurable friction that was just short of pain.

"When do you go back to the doctor? I want to make love to you." His voice was little more than a growl against her neck. He nipped once at the tender flesh, hard enough to make her yelp in surprise. "Don't tell me no again. I've waited a year already."

She didn't want to wait any longer, either. But his mention of the doctor reminded her that it wasn't possible, that she wasn't healed enough yet. She tried to pull away from him but only succeeded in wedging her arms between them when he didn't release her. "Tye, I—*oh, damn!*"

Her shirt was soaked. The tingling she'd felt in her breasts had been her let-down reflex, stimulated by an arousal different from that of her son's suckling, but with the same result. Her breasts were leaking milk like no tomorrow.

Tye still had his arms loosely around her. He was looking down at the large wet circles on the front of her shirt with an annoyingly silly grin on his face. "I guess I'm not the only one who needs a dry shirt."

She knew her face was red. She crossed her arms over her traitorous breasts, clamping her forearms firmly against her breasts to stop the let-down just as Tye placed a gentle finger under her chin, lifting her face to his.

"Don't be embarrassed—it's natural."

"I know. It's just..."

"Want some help getting cleaned up?" His suggestive smile left no doubt about what he intended, and her head immediately filled with an image of his head bending closer, his firm lips seeking her ultrasensitive nipples....

"No!" Her voice came out more sharply than she'd meant it to. "I'm not going to get involved with you, Tye."

His eyes grew watchful though he continued to smile. "We're already involved. But we'll wait until after we're married to make love, if that makes you feel better."

"Ryan isn't even six weeks old, so we can't, anyway," she snapped. Then she realized what she'd said implied acceptance. "And I already told you I'm not going to marry you, so it's a moot point!"

A muscle worked in his cheek. Before she could move away from the danger zone, he grabbed her by the shoulders and dragged her to him again, dropping his head and punishing her lips with a fierce, bruising kiss that took without waiting for her to offer. "You want me. I want you. We have a son, and dammit, you are going to marry me."

Releasing her so suddenly that she nearly fell, he spun on his heel and stomped away.

Six

___

Up and down, up and down. Her arm was beginning to ache from the unaccustomed motion, but Dulcie was determined to finish painting the second side of the henhouse before lunch. It probably would have been easier, and faster, to roll it on, but the surface of the weathered old building was so uneven that she'd have had to go over it with a brush, anyway.

She wondered how Ryan was doing. Angel had volunteered to watch him and to let her know when he got hungry. She'd fed him once already since breakfast, and if her timing was right, he might be ready for his lunch feeding about the time she went in for a break and a sandwich.

The maternal thing certainly was funny. Here she was, not a hundred yards from the house, fretting about her baby. Angel was doing a wonderful job, no doubt. But Angel wasn't Ryan's mother. There was just no substitute for the real thing—although Ryan might not mind being left, she certainly minded leaving. All morning she'd had to fight the urge to check on her son, to quit what she was doing and simply go and be with him.

Just as she was fighting the urge to be with his daddy.

Deliberately, she turned her gaze away from the corral where it had wandered. On the other side of that fence, Tye was trimming the hooves of several of the horses in the ranch's string. All morning, she'd forced herself not to glance at him, not to think of him. All morning, she'd found that despite her best efforts, her eyes seemed to think they were a compass and he was the magnetic pole.

If only he wasn't so appealing. If only he wasn't so good with Ryan.

If only her body didn't try to double-cross her resolve every time she was with him. Her mind knew he was wrong for her, but every time he walked into a room, her body shouted that he was oh, so right.

But he wasn't.

How could she forget the misery she'd felt during her marriage? The deep hurt she'd suffered when she finally realized her husband, whom she'd loved and trusted completely, had been unfaithful? The shock and rage when she'd figured out that she hadn't been the only woman in Lyle's bed for a very long time, if ever?

Only a fool would repeat the mistake of marrying a man who would be away so much. Only a fool would invite heartbreak. The problem was, she thought, her gaze on the man so competently working in the corral, she was already halfway to heartbreak now. And she guessed that made her a first-class fool.

It would be better to stop it before it really got started. Whether she liked it or not, her feelings for Tye were much different from her feelings for Lyle. Much stronger.

If Tye betrayed her, she wouldn't survive it.

A movement in the corral caught her attention, then she dropped her paint brush and lurched toward the fence. The Appaloosa mare apparently hadn't liked Tye's technique; she'd just kicked him squarely in the chest.

Tye was rolling in the dust clutching his chest when she climbed the fence and dropped into the dirt beside him. After doing a skittish dance across the dirt, the Appaloosa was swatting flies with her tail on the other side of the corral, looking as pleased as a horse could look.

"Let me look at you," she said, trying to pull his hands aside so that she could get to his torso.

Tye choked, then broke into a spasm of coughing with his arms wrapped around his chest, and she began to feel really alarmed. She'd heard of men being kicked in the heart, horror stories about them dying right on the spot. She shoved him onto his back and grasped at his hands again, yanking them apart.

They moved so easily that she fell face-forward. Her bottom tilted into the air and her nose landed somewhere in the region of his throat.

His chest was still heaving beneath her. Belatedly, she realized he was laughing. *Laughing*, when she thought he was mortally wounded.

"You rat!" She balled her fist and slugged him in the shoulder. "I thought you were hurt."

"Hey, I am," he protested, grabbing her fists before she could hit him again. "Wait a minute, I— *hey!*" He dodged as she pulled her fist free and flailed at him again. In a lithe moment of strength, he jackknifed and twisted, pulling her beneath him and pinning her arms to the ground.

Abruptly she was furious. A rage that she didn't know she possessed was unleashed from somewhere deep within her, and she heaved and twisted, gritting her teeth and kicking to dislodge him. After his first surprised exclamation, Tye stopped grinning and concentrated on waiting her out, holding her just firmly enough that she couldn't escape him.

When she finally stopped fighting him, she was sobbing with spent fury. Tears trickled from the corners of her eyes and slipped back into her hair.

"Duls?" Tye's voice sounded as if he weren't sure whether she would explode again. "Did I do something to make you mad?"

She opened her mouth to answer him and was mortified when a sob escaped. "I don't know. I thought you were hurt... I was terrified... and then you *laughed....*" Another sob rose in her throat and she

swallowed thickly. "Please let me up. I have to go inside."

He moved off her, then, helping her to her feet and
brushing the dust from her clothing. But he didn't let
go of her hand. "I'm sorry if I scared you. All I could
think about was what I must have looked like getting
knocked off my stool like that." His grin was back,
but it died when she didn't respond.

He pulled loose the first few snaps on his shirt, and
she could see the large, purpling bruise the mare's hoof
had left. Strangely enough, the sight almost reduced
her to tears again.

"You need to put some ice on that," she told him as
she rose, intent on escape. "I'll send some out."

"Hey, Tye! You gotta learn to dodge faster." He
wanted to go after Dulcie, but her brother was hob-
bling across the packed earth toward him, a huge grin
on his face.

Tye removed his shirt and used it to dust himself
off. "You talking about the horse or the woman?"

Day hooted with laughter. "Looked to me like both
of 'em got the best of you."

"Is that what you came all the way out here to tell
me?" He stalked off toward the barn, not caring if
Day couldn't keep up with him. He was in no mood to
be hassled.

"Nope. I—ouch, dammit, slow down!" Day put
too much weight on his injured leg and had to hop for
a few steps.

"If you'd use those crutches the doctor gave you,
that thing might have a chance to heal."

"I am healing. I'll be back in the saddle next week. Now do you want to hear what I have to say about buying a ranch or not?"

Tye slowed down a hair. "Buying what ranch?"

When Day didn't answer, he slowed even more, turning to look at the other man. Day was grinning. "Thought you might be interested."

"Can't say until I hear, can I?"

"Guess not." Day's grin was eating up his face. "Ol' guy who owned the spread that adjoins mine died a few months back. Had no close family and he left the land to a niece from back East."

"And?"

Day leaned against the fence, adjusting his weight to give his damaged leg a rest. "Niece came out to look at the place last week. I just heard she took one look and told the solicitor to call a realtor." He paused. "Since it's in my best interest to get my sister out of my hair, and you might be my last chance to do it, thought I'd better pass it on." He fished in his pocket and extended a slip of paper to Tye, who reached for it slowly.

Day might have sounded casual, but Tye knew better. Dulcie's brother had accepted him. He folded the paper and tucked it into his own pocket. "Thanks for the tip." As he turned away, Day cleared his throat.

"You two still, uh, negotiating?"

Tye shrugged, slinging his shirt over his shoulder. "Heck if I know. Woman's got me so confused I'm not sure whether I'm comin' or goin'."

Day grinned and slapped him companionably on the shoulder before he turned and began to limp back in the direction of the house. "Sounds like things are goin' just fine. They don't bother makin' you crazy unless they care."

Ryan was cooing, his little hands and legs waving madly, scrunching up the soft woven blanket on which Tye had laid him. The muted turquoise was a perfect foil for the baby's soft flesh, dappled by the spotty shade underneath the cottonwood where Tye had placed it. He glanced toward the house, where Dulcie already was starting the evening meal. She'd been polite but distant when he'd asked if he could take Ryan out for a while, just as she'd been ever since that scene in the corral yesterday.

What had been going through her head? He'd thought they were having some lighthearted fun; she'd been intent on killing him there for a few moments. What had happened? The blind rage that had possessed her was far too intense for the small trick he'd played, letting her think he was hurt. And yet the thought had reduced her to tears.

Was it possible she was beginning to care for him? The notion produced a warmth inside him, but it died quickly when he thought of her behavior since then. She'd been treating him like he had the plague.

And yet he couldn't shake the idea that she felt more kindly to him than she was letting on. How could she kiss him the way she'd kissed him in the barn the other day if she didn't care for him at least a little? Was it just a physical thing?

That kiss. He was starting to think of it as a cross he might have to bear for the rest of his life if Dulcie wouldn't marry him. Every time he touched her, she went up in flames like dry land in a brushfire. She had thrown herself into kissing him with the same passion she'd shown him the night they'd created Ryan, a passion she'd worked hard to avoid ever since. Just thinking about it made him hot.

And all he did was think about it. The way her sweetly rounded bottom fit into his palms, the way she opened her legs just a little bit, the way he fit into that opening just enough to feel how it would be when he had her naked and begging him for it again.... Hell, yesterday, she'd been sobbing beneath him and for a brief moment, he'd considered coaxing her out of it with a kiss, sliding his body down to cover hers....

He groaned aloud, willing himself to quit thinking of Dulcie, willing his body to forget how badly it wanted to plunge into her waiting warmth.

How could she just pretend that kiss never happened? She had to be the most cantankerous woman in the whole Southwest. Except for trying to take his head off, she hadn't given him the time of day since they'd practically crawled down each other's throat in the barn the day he'd pulled that calf. A brief satisfaction at the memory of the heifer and calf, who had both survived to trot around the ranch another day, disappeared when he thought of how she'd been treating him.

He wasn't some old boot to be tried on and recycled when it didn't fit. He was a man, with feelings and needs. And amen to the needs.

Ryan squawked, interrupting his moment of satisfying self-pity. He'd better concentrate on these photos or Ryan would be nothing but a dark blur and Dulcie would wonder what he'd been doing. Securing the camera on the tripod, he squinted into the viewfinder and tried several f-stops until he got the light right. Better hurry now, before the sun moved or the baby got fussy.

It was late afternoon, and he'd knocked off a little early because he'd realized yesterday that he had to get some shots of Ryan outdoors. He could envision exactly what the finished print would reveal...except that his photographs never lived up to the glorious image in his head. A few came close, but the majority of them, critically acclaimed as they were, didn't satisfy him.

That thought was an echo of those running through his head in the past couple of hours. Ever since Day had mentioned that Harley Moser's niece had inherited the ranch that adjoined his, and that she was looking for a buyer.

Hearing those words, he'd recognized something within himself that he'd never known before.

He loved ranching. It was the reason why he'd been dissatisfied with the thought of roaming around the West anymore. The time he'd spent working the land again, first in Montana and now down here, had soothed his soul in a way his photography never had.

He'd been running away from it for almost thirty years now, but the simple truth was that he'd been born to the land, and unless he accepted that, some very important part of his life was going to pass him by, only to rear its head and hiss at him when he was eighty and too old to start again.

The shutter clicked several times, recording his son. His son. Those two little words never failed to awe him. He wanted roots, dammit, and he wanted land and traditions that he could pass on to his son. In short, all those things that represented the security denied him as a child.

But security was more than a plot of soil, more than a way of doing things and a sense of where you came from. Security was family, and in that he'd been luckier than most people he knew. Ryan deserved that. Maybe if she knew he wouldn't uproot her, if she knew she could depend on him to stick close and ride his own range, she'd consent to marry him. She'd have to, wouldn't she? Ryan would get a father and she would get a husband who wouldn't always be leaving.

He could do that! The thought of a ranch of his own was so exciting that his hands shook on the camera. He could still take photos whenever he wanted, but he'd be a rancher. Not somebody's relative, not somebody's foreman, but a rancher with a spread of his own and honest-to-God New Mexico dust and grit under his fingernails. Tumbleweed, bawling cattle and unbroken colts ... all his.

A horrible thought interrupted his idyll. What if Moser's niece had already found a buyer? A hell of a thought!

He sprang to his feet, glancing at his watch. If he called now, he could get his lawyer working on an offer before the business day ended. Full of plans and excitement, he turned and started for the house. A second later, he remembered Ryan. And his camera. Swearing, he whipped around and snatched the baby up so fast that his little mouth quivered and puckered up to howl.

"Now you just cut out that bawling, son," Tye crooned as he juggled the baby and unscrewed the camera from the tripod. "Your daddy's going to make everything right real soon."

"I went to the doctor for my six-week checkup today."

Holding her breath, she watched Tye lift his head from the stock magazine he'd been reading after dinner. They were alone in the family room, since Day and Angel had gone up to bed when they'd tucked in Beth Ann. She knew they had a television and a sitting area in their big bedroom, but she was beginning to feel somewhat guilty about running them out of their own living area every evening. It was as if they didn't want to intrude.

Not that there was anything to intrude on. Each evening, she and Tye sat like two bumps on a pickle, attending to Ryan and carefully avoiding each other.

Tye looked across the length of the couch at her, but she couldn't read his expression. "Are you healthy?"

"As a horse." She dropped her eyes to Ryan, who was cycling his legs erratically in her lap. "I'm officially allowed to do anything I like."

"Good." He hesitated as if he was going to add something, then shook his head almost imperceptibly and rose. "I guess I'll turn in. G'night."

Good night? "Good night."

Three hours later, she lay staring at the ceiling in her darkened bedroom.

Her face was still burning with . . . humiliation was what it was. Tye hadn't rushed to pick up on her unspoken message when she'd oh-so-casually mentioned her six-week checkup. He'd darn near leaped to his feet and run from the room, in fact. She'd worried her feelings around all day, had nearly driven right off the side of the road on the way home thinking about Tye, and all he could say was "Good."

She hadn't invited him here. She hadn't asked him to hang around under her feet until she couldn't ignore him. She hadn't asked him to kiss her senseless, or to make her want him so badly she could barely look at him without begging him to take her somewhere private and lie down with her.

Restlessly, she flung off the light sheet that covered her, sat up and reached for the glass of water on her nightstand. It was empty.

She felt like throwing the glass against the wall and damn the noise, but she'd never been one to give in to impulse—at least, until she met Tye—and she wasn't going to give in now.

Rising, she picked up the glass and padded barefoot out of her bedroom and down the hall. In the kitchen, she refilled her glass and leaned against the counter, sipping. She'd been able to think of nothing but Tye since the day she'd thought he was injured by that horse.

It had shaken her up, thinking that he had been badly hurt. And when he'd laughed, something had just snapped inside her. She'd wanted to scream at him for not caring, for treating her feelings as if they were disposable.

They weren't disposable! How could he just expect her to turn off her love for him—

Love. Doggone it. She hadn't planned on that. It had been dancing around in her head for days now, and she'd been firmly sidestepping the thought every time, deliberately tuning out what her own heart was trying to tell her. She'd been fighting it since they'd met, refusing to acknowledge that her neighbor and friend could be far, far more; since he'd come to find her at the ranch, she'd been *running* from her feelings.

She loved him. There was a sweet flood of satisfaction at merely being able to acknowledge it. For the first time, she could pull out mental images of Tye as she'd seen him around the ranch in the past few weeks, and allow herself the luxury of lingering over each detail of his hard physique, recalling her fascination with the movements of his lips when he spoke, the quirk of a dimple in his chin and the way he tossed one errant lock of hair off his forehead when he was concentrating on getting a photograph set up just so.

Carrying her glass, she left the kitchen and started back up the stairs. At the top, she hesitated at the door of her own bedroom, then passed it by and moved on down the hall to Ryan's room. When she'd first brought him home from the hospital, he'd slept right in her bed. It had been an easy arrangement for them both while he'd been getting himself into some kind of schedule. But very quickly, more quickly than she had expected, he'd begun sleeping for five- and six-hour stretches at night, and she'd moved him to his crib in the nursery, knowing she would sleep better if he wasn't beside her. It seemed that every time he rustled or twitched or made the slightest peep, she was wide awake, wondering if he was all right.

The small night-light in Ryan's room gave plenty of light. She stood by the crib for a few moments, feeling a rush of love well up inside her for the tiny person whose little body was limp and content in slumber.

Then a change in the air, more a feeling than a sound, alerted her that she wasn't alone. Turning, she saw Tye's broad shoulders framed in the doorway. As he crossed to her side, he whispered, "Is he okay?"

She smiled, watching as he put his hands on the crib rail and bent to get a closer look at his sleeping son. "He's fine," she said in an equally soft tone, but she was no longer thinking of the baby. Her heart had begun to beat faster and her breath was coming quicker at the sight of the man she loved.

Tye wore no shirt. His jeans looked as if they had been hastily donned; while the zipper was pulled up, the garment was unbuttoned at the top and the edges fell open to reveal a line of tight curls arrowing straight down from the tight little whorl of his navel. She was stunned to realize how badly she wanted to lower that zipper and touch him, to turn into his arms and know again the wild passion that they'd shared the night they'd created the baby who slept so peacefully before them.

"Duls?" Tye turned and looked down at her. His voice was deeper, huskier than usual, and in one heated flash of understanding, she knew that he felt it, too—this strange, irresistible attraction that drew them together.

She moved slowly, laying her hand tenderly atop his where it rested on the edge of the crib. With her other hand, she reached up and cupped his cheek in her palm.

Tye looked surprised, but it only took him an instant to recover. He turned his head and pressed his lips into her palm at the same time that his hand came up and rested at her waist, exerting a light, gentle pressure, just enough to draw her in against the hard warmth of his half-naked body.

Contentment flowed through her. She relaxed, resting her head against the solid muscle of his chest, and exhaled a long sigh of delight. This was where she belonged. Why had it taken her so long to admit it? Beneath her ear, she could hear his heart beating, the sound muted and reassuring. Her hand left its place on his and traveled up to rest on the smooth silky skin at the joint of his shoulder; when he lifted his own hand and brought it to rest with its brother at her back, the glide of muscle beneath the skin was a tactile pleasure almost too great to bear.

Slowly she turned her head and pressed her face against him, taking deep breaths of the musky, arousing unmistakable male scent of his body. Her lips moved blindly, pressing wet, openmouthed kisses on the smooth flesh of his chest. She felt so safe here, so...cared for. He was much taller than she. Above her head, she could hear the muscles of his throat work as he swallowed. Then his head bent, sliding down across her hair, hot breath whispering over her cheek, nuzzling along with unshakable purpose until he found her mouth.

She gave a small sound, really a squeak, of sheer shock at the electric sensation that ran through her when his lips slid firmly onto hers. Her toes curled and so did her body, pressing into him in blatant invitation. He kissed her with devastating thoroughness, playing with her lips before gently conquering her with his tongue. Leisurely he explored her mouth, holding her loosely with his arms around her waist, using his mouth to communicate wordlessly his need for her.

Wrapping her arms around his neck, she gave her body to him. Her breasts pressed into his chest, her stomach recorded the searing imprint of his arousal. A guttural growl tore from his throat, and he slipped his palms purposefully down her back to palm her bottom, lifting her until her toes dangled off the ground and both of them gasped at the sudden, snug fit of sex to sex.

She wriggled against him, each small movement telegraphing its message of need from the flashpoint of her aching body. Her hand left his neck and moved down between their bodies, needing to touch him, to explore the hard, pulsing length of flesh. The open button yielded to her mission and she slipped her hand into the front of his jeans, making a small sound of delight as she realized he hadn't worn underwear. Crisp curls tantalized for an instant, and then she found him, filling her hand with his hot, silky flesh, gripping and caressing him until his breath was whistling in and out between his teeth like the tortured engine of a train pushed beyond its limits.

"Whoa, there," he breathed against her mouth, catching her by the wrist and drawing her hand away from his body. Relaxing his grip on her bottom, he allowed her to slide down to stand on her toes, though he still bore the weight of her.

"Don't you want me?" She already knew the answer. She'd felt it for herself.

"You know I do." He was panting but the merest hint of steel shone for a moment through his measured tones. "But this time, I want to be sure you know what you're doing."

"I do know!"

"Do you?" He dropped her wrist and placed his hands on either side of her face, cupping her jaw and forcing her to look at him. "I'm not your personal release valve, Dulcie. If I take you to bed tonight, I want you to be damned sure you know who I am."

The intensity of his voice forced his words into her consciousness like bullets into a wall. She stood motionless between his hands for a long moment. Then, reaching up to encircle his wrists with her own, she looked deep into his eyes. "I've always known who you were, Tye. You're dedicated, unselfish, chivalrous—all the things that I find most appealing. Do you think I would have made love with you otherwise?"

Silence enshrouded them in a thick curtain. Her body was throbbing out its message of need, urging her to show him what he meant to her. But tension flowed from him in an almost tangible current. This time had to be his decision. Slowly, she released his wrists and stepped back, keeping her gaze on his face. She felt as if she were facing a firing squad.

When his face changed, the relief almost knocked her to her knees. If this was what truly loving someone did to you, she wasn't sure she liked it.

Tye stepped forward so that their bodies were touching again and the sweet sensation made her close her eyes. She felt his breath whisper over her skin and his gentle kiss on her forehead. "Open your eyes," he said. "When I make love to you, we're both going to have our eyes open this time."

Seven

He felt like the king of the universe as he lifted her into his arms and carried her from their son's room across the hall into his. She clung to his neck while he shut the door and locked it. Then he carried her across to the big bed where he'd been sleeping alone and set her on her feet beside it.

"May I undress you?"

"Please." Her voice was a throaty whisper, and she lifted her arms docilely to assist him with removing the modest cotton gown she wore.

As he tossed the gown aside, he tried in vain to get enough air into suddenly burning lungs. How could he have forgotten how beautifully she was made? She had worn no panties beneath the gown, and all her lush secrets were revealed. Her breasts had been generous even before the baby. Now, ripe with milk and motherhood, they bounced gently against her slender torso, the large, dusky nipples beckoning him to sample their bounty. Her waist was already regaining its shape, and her hips, flared and womanly, framed the black thicket of curls between her legs.

He shuddered, so aroused by the mere sight of her that he was afraid if he touched her he'd lose all self-control. Deep breaths, he told himself. Deep, deep breaths.

Then he forgot to breathe at all as she stepped forward and placed her hands at the zipper of his jeans. "Now it's my turn," she said, smiling up at him as she pulled the tab steadily downward.

In her smile was the feminine knowledge of how she affected him, and suddenly, as his sex sprang free of the confining fabric, he couldn't wait to touch her. His hands lifted of their own will, shaping themselves to the smooth, cool mounds of her breasts, chafing the tender nipples with his thumbs until her breasts warmed beneath his touch. She cried out and her hands fell away from his body.

He caught her beneath the arms as she swayed toward him, but he didn't lay her down. Holding her in place with one arm behind her back, arching her body up for his intimate appraisal, he bent his head to her breasts.

Just before his mouth closed over one ripe crest, he glanced up at her. "Is it all right?"

Her eyes were closed and her head was thrown back, but she nodded.

And then, as he closed his mouth over the rigid tip, her whole body jerked in response. He pulled strongly at her breast, tonguing the turgid nipple, suckling the milky sustenance that fed his son, and she moaned. Swiveling, he eased himself down onto the side of the bed with her still arched across his arm. His free hand kneaded her other breast, tugging at the tip before sliding down across her body, enjoying the silken texture of her abdomen, combing gently through the curls between her legs, teasing apart the humid folds of feminine flesh until his probing fingers found moisture. Her hips rose and fell once, then again and again as he dipped his fingers into her small well and then, slick with her essence, sought out the tiny bud that gave her pleasure. As her hips rotated, revolved, revelled in his touch, his erection surged against her satiny buttock, receiving her unintentional caresses with growing insistence.

She was breathing in shallow, panting rhythms now, her sweet cleft rolling up to meet each stroke. Faster and faster she moved; he felt the juices of his own body creating an even sweeter friction against her hip and he groaned aloud. Her hands flailed, gripping the sheets, his leg, anything, as her head rolled blindly. Then she flung a hand to her mouth, biting back a scream as uncontrollable, shuddering surges of climax took her, arching her back repeatedly, stimulating him to madness.

Her body was still heaving in the grip of ecstasy as he shifted her upright and spread her legs with his own, grabbing her by both hips and pulling her down,

down, arching himself up to meet her, pushing himself into her in a frenzy. He sucked in a hot breath of joy at the tight, sweet wetness that welcomed him in its clasp. Bucking, blinded and shaking with need, he thrust to his own desperate finish as her flesh quivered and clung around him.

When the mists receded and he finally had enough breath to lift his head, she was curled limply against him, her head lolling against his shoulder.

"How in the hell," he gasped out, "did we manage…to keep…our hands off each other for so long?"

He felt the little chuckle shake her. "Willpower?"

He let himself down to the bed, one elbow at a time, with her still draped over him and his flesh still snugly within her. "I have no willpower where you're concerned. If I had, I never would have gotten involved with another man's wife."

She tensed. "I wasn't another man's wife when we got involved."

He stroked a lazy hand down her back, soothing her. "I don't mean the first time we…did this. I was talking about the first time I saw you unlocking the door to your apartment. I knew you were a married woman, but I waltzed on over and talked to you, anyway."

She had raised her head from his shoulder and was staring down at him with wide eyes. "You were attracted to me then?"

He grinned, enjoying the way her hair fell around them, creating their own little tent of intimacy. "Don't look so surprised. You're hardly the Wicked Witch of the West." Raising a hand, he gently pressed her head back to his shoulder, where it belonged. "I admit, at first I had lecherous thoughts of a quick seduction, but after we went out to dinner that first time, I realized you weren't the kind of woman who wears one man's ring while having a fling with another."

"So you took the high road and became my friend." She yawned. "Oops, sorry."

Reaching out with one arm, he groped around for the covers, wondering if it would be possible to get her into his bed without moving her off him. Sitting up, he held her in place with one arm beneath her buttocks while he stood and kicked his jeans the rest of the way off. Then, without ever releasing her—or even more to his liking, without her releasing him—he eased himself down into the bed and lay down with her still comfortably resting atop him. "I think I prefer this to friendship."

She moved her hips, measuring how much he preferred it. "I think I agree."

Turning his head, he captured her lips, kissing her thoroughly before rolling so that she was beneath him. "Know what else I think?"

"What?" Her eyes danced; she knew the answer.

"I think I'd like to do this again."

Ryan was fussing. Shaking her head to clear the sleepiness, she sat up. As her eyes adjusted to the darkness, she realized that she wasn't in her own bed.

And she remembered why. But when she turned her head to confirm Tye's presence, he wasn't there. A swift glance at the clock showed her it was still only the middle of the night. Three o'clock. Time for Ryan to eat.

She shifted to the side of the bed, but before she could rise, the bedroom door opened. In the glow from the small lamp in the hallway, she could see that it was Tye and that he was carrying Ryan. "Here he is, changed and ready to guzzle." Closing the door behind him, he came around to the side of the bed and held out a damp cloth. "Thought you might like to use this before you nurse him."

Even in the dark, she knew he was grinning. Thank God he couldn't see the blush she could feel spreading up across her cheeks. "Thank you." Quickly, she bathed her breasts. Then, she took Ryan, sitting up and preparing herself to nurse him. Tye came around the other side of the big bed and slid in behind her, pulling her back to lean against his chest while she breast-fed his son. "Isn't this nice?" he said into her ear.

She ducked her head in answer, her heart too full for response. Yes, it was nice. She wished every day of her life could be like this. Tye was all she had ever wanted in a man . . . when he was around.

But he wasn't around all the time. And much as she wanted to fool herself, she knew that a life with Tye would never work. He was the wrong kind of man.

He returned Ryan to the crib for her when she had finished the feeding. She debated going back to her own room while he was gone. It would be wiser, even though every cell in her body cried out to her to stay.

But before she could make up her mind, Tye came back into the room. He got into bed and pulled her into the curve of his body as naturally as if they had slept this way for years.

"The opening of my show in Santa Fe is next Saturday," he said into her ear. "I'd like to get there on Thursday. That'll give me time to check everything out and maybe have time to rent some darkroom space on Friday. I want to develop some prints of the stuff I've taken here on the ranch." When she didn't respond, he went on. "We can have room service as much as you like so you don't have to worry about taking Ryan into restaurants. You won't need much in the way of dress clothes. Just something for the opening." He chuckled. "Something light colored, so when Ryan spits up, he won't ruin a nice little black dress."

She stirred restlessly, all too aware that normally he would be leaving her to do this. "I'm not sure that taking Ryan and me along is such a good idea."

He was quiet for a moment. "Why not?"

"I just don't." She knew she sounded unreasonable, bullheaded, and she waited for Tye's temper to stir.

But he didn't get angry. Instead, he bombarded her with logic. "As Ryan gets older, he's going to have a million and one questions for each of us. He'll grow up here learning ranching, but eventually he'll want to know about my career in photography. How can you answer his questions if you haven't experienced it?"

She wanted to cry, but she wouldn't. Especially not while he was holding her in his arms, waiting for her response. He might want her to marry him so that Ryan could have a name, but already he was making plans for them to go their separate ways. That much was obvious, if he wasn't even going to be around enough to answer Ryan's questions himself.

Apparently, he took her silence for the continued refusal it was, because he took another breath and spoke again, his breath stirring the hair near her temple. "The ranch is a wonderful place for Ryan to grow up. But I'm not sure it's the best place for you."

She pulled herself from his arms and sat up, looking over her shoulder at him indignantly. "Why not?"

"You don't just live here because you love it," he said, holding her gaze in the dim light that was beginning to creep in around the edges of the drawn curtains. "You use it as a place to hide from the world."

"That's not true! I live here because I love the freedom and the wide-open space. I lived in the city long enough to know it holds no appeal for me. I'm not a city kind of girl."

"So you only live here because you enjoy the lifestyle?"

"That's what I just said, isn't it?" Her chin came up. "I can go to town anytime I want. I simply choose to live in this world most of the time."

"I guess I was wrong about thinking you're afraid to leave this ranch."

"You betcha."

"And I was wrong in thinking that you were afraid to go to Santa Fe with me."

"You were." Too late, she saw the trap.

"So you'll go?"

The rat. The last thing she wanted to do was spend days cooped up in a hotel room with him, growing to care for him more and more...and he knew it. But she'd been outmaneuvered at every turn. "Oh, all right, I'll go." It was less than gracious, but she wasn't going to pretend she was thrilled about this little trip.

She started to flounce out of the bed, but he caught her by the waist and tumbled her back to the mattress, settling his weight on her. "Where are you going?"

"It's time to get up." She pushed against his chest without any noticeable effect. Deep in her belly, a quivering awareness responded to the rough male thighs that forced hers wide.

"No, it's not." He dropped his head and kissed her leisurely, until she abandoned her posture of indifference and wound her arms around his neck, kissing him back and arching her body into his. He raised his head a fraction and she braced herself to see triumph on his face, but instead he was looking down at her with an odd, unreadable light in his hazel eyes. "This is how I want us to start every day of our married lives."

I can't marry you! her mind shouted. But as he lowered his head to claim her lips again, she forgot why it was so important to tell him so.

She'd been to Santa Fe many times before, but as Tye drove through the city, she had the feeling she'd never really seen it before. Albuquerque had been brash, bustling, a jarring mix of the rough sensibilities of the Old West and the slick packaging of contemporary society. Santa Fe, on the other hand, reminded her of a perfectly put together lady.

Her narrow streets were host to Southwestern artists who soaked up her ambience and committed it to tangible form for the thousands of tourists who came seeking authenticity. In Albuquerque, the sun had seemed harsh and unforgiving at times. In Santa Fe, the light seemed somehow right. It enhanced every stone it touched.

Perhaps it wasn't the location. It seemed unfair to compare Albuquerque, scene of her life's most miserable moments, to Santa Fe. This city would always linger haloed in her memory by the mere fact that she had come here with Tye.

She felt new, as if she'd been born yesterday. Only a year ago, she had been miserably unhappy, lonely, cleaning her spotless apartment and pretending she didn't care that her marriage had unraveled. Now she was the mother of a son, the lover of another man who wanted her more than she'd ever dreamed she could be wanted.

She was happy. It was a shock to realize it.

And equally important not to forget how easily it could all turn to dust.

She glanced across the seat at Tye. His forearms were tanned and muscular where they were bared by the rolled-up sleeves of his shirt. Long, strong, lean-fingered hands competently maneuvered the car through the narrow streets; she felt a tug of awareness bloom deep in her abdomen, and her body grew slack with anticipation. Those hands had been over every inch of her body in the past two nights. She had no reason to doubt they wouldn't explore her as thoroughly this evening.

Tye caught her gazing at him, and his eyes deepened to the color of topaz. "What are you thinking about?"

"Nothing." But she knew her face had grown red. He chuckled, sliding a hand across the seat to clasp over hers where they lay in her lap. "Liar."

His fingers curled around hers, sliding against her thigh, and she nearly jumped out of her seat. The urge to lift her hips slightly and capture his fingers between her thighs hit her like the hard, jarring fall from a horse, leaving her gasping for oxygen. Feeling desperate, she twined her fingers between his and lifted their joined hands to the seat between them.

"I can't marry you," she blurted. Despite her happiness, it was best to keep that clear between them.

His fingers tensed for a moment, then relaxed, as if he'd had to think about it. "You worry too much. Why don't we just forget about the M-word for a while?"

Easy for him to say. He had never felt the helpless despair, the loss of intimacy that accompanied the demise of a marriage. He had never cried himself to sleep when a partnership he'd expected to last forever fell apart.

She resented the way he made it seem so logical. So what if they were a fantastic physical match? You couldn't spend your whole life in bed. Sooner or later, this clawing need inside her would fade to a more manageable glow.

Wouldn't it? She had a sudden image of two elderly people tearing at each other's clothes as they sat side by side in their wheelchairs and bit back the bubble of laughter that rose. Thankfully, Tye pulled the car to a stop in front of their hotel at that moment, and she was diverted by practical decisions and needs.

The hotel was one of the city's most exclusive. Tye waved the bellboy aside and hefted their bags himself. She followed with Ryan, wondering if he'd signed them in as his family, or if the desk clerk knew she wasn't his wife.

As they stepped off the elevator, she erased the last thought. If she was going to be single for the rest of her life, she'd better get past caring what other people thought.

The suite was gorgeous. She didn't even want to guess at how much the two bedrooms separated by a central living area would cost. A crib had already been installed in one of the bedrooms. Tye dumped his bag in one bedroom and headed for the telephone, where she heard him double-checking his arrangements for darkroom space and for the reception.

She felt funny watching him place her suitcase alongside his duffel bag in the larger of the two bedrooms, but she couldn't bring herself to say anything.

Besides, what would she have said?

By the time she had unpacked and hung up her things, Ryan was getting fussy on his blanket on the bed. Tye stuck his head into the bedroom long enough to tell her he was going to work in his darkroom for a few hours.

"Why don't you take a nap?" he suggested, drawing her into his arms for a quick kiss. "Think of this as a vacation. You have nothing else to do but take care of Ryan and let me take care of you."

Then he was gone. Ryan was beginning to be more than just mildly unhappy, and she changed his diaper before settling down in a comfortable chair to feed him. As he nursed, his tiny hands kneaded her breast. Looking down at her son, she could see a fierce scowl of concentration contorting his features. It was so like the way Tye looked when he was fiddling with his cameras that she had to hold back laughter.

How could she have considered keeping Ryan a secret from his father?

It was clear, now that she had the luxury of looking back, that she'd been dead wrong. She carried Ryan to the crib and returned to the huge, king-size bed in the master bedroom. Tye was right. She was tired. She'd sleep for an hour or so and be up again before he returned....

Hands. Strong, soothing hands moved over her, stroking, smoothing out the fabric bunched around her. The room was cooler than she was accustomed to, and she snuggled deep into the covers, enjoying the heat they generated. She dreamed that Tye was coming to her, and in her dream she threw her arms about his neck, kissing him with uninhibited joy as he bore her down onto a bed of scented grass. His body surged against hers and a hot arrow of desire rushed to the center between her legs, making her moan and draw him closer. His mouth closed over her tender nipple and she cried out, pulling his head hard against her—

And in the space between one heartbeat and the next, she came awake. Tye's hands were racing over her, stroking, smoothing, squeezing her flesh in the secret places that longed for his touch. His lips tugged at her and her body responded, every muscle in her going slack and loose with desire. She was wet, and growing wetter. When she whispered that in his ear, a mighty groan tore from his throat. He pushed her onto her back and placed himself between her legs in one continuous motion, groaning again when she reached between them and guided him to that needy, liquid-slicked place. He took her thighs in his hands; as he surged forward, burying himself within her, he pulled her legs up to drape over his shoulders. She whimpered at the delicious feeling. Her back arched and she clasped her ankles behind his head. He was moving against her, a storm breaking against her shore, wave after wave pounding her exposed beachhead until the storm broke over her head in a ragged crescendo of force and fury. She screamed and his mouth caught the sound as her body shuddered beneath him. Then his own body stiffened and thrust in answer, emptying his seed into the receptive welcome of her love.

They drifted for a long while. She lightly ran her fingernails up and down his back, and against her hair, he heaved a sigh of contentment. After a time, he pulled his body from her and rolled onto his back, dragging her with him to cuddle into his side. She laid her head against his shoulder and allowed him to turn her onto her side against him, extending her arm as far as it would reach across his wide chest. "Welcome back."

Above her head, he cleared his throat. "That was some kind of welcome. Are you always that enthusiastic?"

She smiled against his chest, turning her head to press a kiss against the solid muscle. "Why don't you stick around and find out, cowboy?"

He hesitated for a second, but in that second, the mood changed. "Oh, I'm planning on it," he said. Then, before she could react to the grim intent ringing in his voice, he rolled again, pinning her beneath him.

His eyes were fierce as he gazed down into hers, but when she glanced away, he put a finger beneath her chin and tilted her face back up to his. "I didn't use any protection."

She swallowed. "I think it's okay. Breast-feeding is a natural form of birth control, you know."

He grunted. "It's not foolproof." Then he dropped his forehead to rest against hers. "I don't want any more of our children to be conceived out of wedlock."

That stung, whether or not he'd meant it to. But she absolutely refused to get into an argument about marriage with him tonight. "Then we'll just have to be more careful," she said. She pressed another kiss to the muscle just above his left nipple, then slowly circled the taut brown tip with her tongue. "And more creative."

She slipped her hand down his body to the wiry curls below his navel, then followed them down even farther. He was only partially aroused and she gently cupped him, loving the slow, sure leap and pulse of his flesh as he grew to full proportion. She extended one finger beneath the twin globes that fell against his thigh, stroking the tender flesh there, eliciting a harsh indrawn breath.

His hand in her hair stopped her. He wasn't entirely gentle as he dragged her hand away and tossed the covers to the foot of the bed. "You want creative? Okay, we'll do creative."

They lounged in the suite for the rest of the evening, ordering room service and watching old movies. In the morning, Tye carried her into the shower before she was even awake and showed her even more creativity than she'd believed possible.

She'd never thought of herself as an exceptionally sensual woman. No, she'd categorize herself more as practical, down-to-earth, all those unflattering adjectives that, when it came right down to it, meant dull and uninspiring.

But here in Tye's arms, her legs wrapped around his waist and their bodies joined in shivering intimacy while the steaming water poured over them from above, she felt sexy, exciting, alluring.

Together, they tumbled out of the shower stall and dragged the thick white towels over each other.

As she blotted water from his sleek chest and the rippling muscles of his abdomen, she bent and kissed the small brown birthmark near his stomach, the one that he'd given Ryan. "Does anyone else in your family have this?"

With her face turned away from his, she felt, rather than saw, the stillness that came over him.

"No," he said. "I'm the only one. My uncle doesn't remember my mother or anyone else in their family having it, so I've always assumed it came from my father's side of the family."

She rose to her feet and put both arms around him as far as she could reach, hugging him tightly to her, but she didn't say a word. She couldn't. It broke her heart to think of the small boy wondering who his father had been, and why his mother had left him.

His arms came around her and they rocked silently. They were standing naked in the bathroom, their bodies fresh from loving, but comfort was the word of the moment. She felt closer to him than she ever had.

After a time, though, they could hear Ryan beginning to wake and fuss and with a kiss and a grin, Tye drew his arms from around her and offered her a robe.

Then he left her to spend the day working in the darkroom he had rented, with a promise to return before dinner.

Eight

Tye carried Ryan into the gallery where his show had been set up. Dulcie walked at his side, noticing that even with the baby in his arms, he still managed small courtesies like opening doors and gesturing for her to precede him.

She smoothed her ivory suit over her hips, feeling self-conscious as several sets of eyes turned their way. A tall, slender man with silver hair broke away from a group of people and hurried toward them.

"Doggone your hide! It's not like you to be late, Tye. The Baders are interested in—" He stopped in midsentence, apparently realizing for the first time what Tye carried in his arms. "Holy Moses." The man turned to Dulcie with a preoccupied frown. "I'm sorry, ma'am, but you'll have to take that child some-where else. Do you realize who this is?''

Before she could respond, Tye laughed aloud. "McNally, do you realize who *this* is?" As the man raised one elegant silver eyebrow in polite confusion, Tye held the baby under his nose. "Bill McNally, this is my son, Ryan. Ryan, my agent, known to most of the world as simply McNally." Then Tye put a hand at her back, propelling her forward a few steps. "And this is Ryan's mother, Dulcie. Duls, McNally."

McNally was looking at Ryan as if the baby had a horn sprouting from his forehead. He raised bewil-dered eyes to Dulcie, automatically said, "A plea-sure, ma'am," and then, turning to Tye, *"Your son?"*

Another grin split Tye's face. "Yep. Can't you tell?"

McNally eyed the baby, apparently seeking the re-semblance. "I was kiddin' when I talked about woman trouble, but you weren't, were ya? Is this a joke?"

Tye raised his right hand. "Swear to God I'm not kiddin', Mac. Want to hold him?"

McNally took a hasty step backward. "No, no, that's okay. I gotta get back to the Baders. They're considerin' purchasin' *Triple D*." He turned and plunged away through the crowd, looking back at the last moment to toss a command at Tye. "Mingle. And *be nice*."

"Be nice?" She studied Tye. "Sounds as if he's worried."

"I'm always nice."

She gave him a wry look that spoke volumes, and he grinned at her. "Sometimes I get a little impatient when people ask stupid questions."

"Impatient enough to kill the sale?"

He shrugged. "Some of these people don't deserve to have my work."

She laughed. "And here I was beginning to think you didn't have an artistic temperament."

"You want to see my artistic temperament?" He offered her an exaggerated leer, bending to speak into her ear. "How about if I show it to you later?"

A shiver worked its way down her spine as his hot breath tickled her ear, and she turned her head to smile at him from beneath her lashes. "Sounds good to me, cowboy."

He patted her bottom. "It will be, darlin'." Then he straightened with a sigh and surveyed the crowd. "Well, I've got my orders. Are you ready to mingle?"

"No." She had to steel herself not to step back a pace. His voice echoed in her head as he'd introduced her as Ryan's mother, neglecting to mention that she wasn't his wife. "You go ahead. I'd rather just... explore a little. Here—" she held out her arms "—I'll take Ryan." As her gaze met Tye's, she saw the warmth and humor drain from him to be replaced by a cool, aloof look that distanced him from her.

"All right. If that's what you want."

She had to force the words past the sudden, stupid lump in her throat. "That's what I want."

He nodded once in curt dismissal. Without another word, he handed Ryan to her, turned and walked away into the crowd.

The rest of the evening was long and miserable. She walked through the gallery, studying Tye's photographs and listening to the chatter around her, but her heart was hurting. Everything was so wrong between them.

Well, maybe not everything. She had to admit that in bed, there was absolutely nothing that could get more *right*. But people couldn't live in bed.

And they couldn't be married for long without love.

If only Tye loved her. She knew that even without love, they shared something very special, something that she'd never known before. But without love, she wasn't strong enough, or brave enough, to risk her heart again. She couldn't marry a man who didn't love her, didn't need her the way she needed him.

And Tye certainly didn't need her. She had nearly gasped aloud when she'd seen the prices discreetly affixed to some of the photographs on display. And nearly all of them had been turned over with equally discreet Sold signs replacing the prices as the evening wore on. She couldn't even guess how much money Tye made in a year, but it was obvious he was far out of her league. A wave of longing for the familiar environment of the ranch swept over her. She fit in there; she belonged.

She watched Tye across the room as he drifted from one knot of people to the next, bending his head to listen to something a heavily made up blonde in a tight halter top was saying. The woman ran long, painted fingernails down his back as she spoke, and his teeth flashed white against his tan when he smiled down at her before moving out of range.

The memory of her apartment, of her husband with another woman, rose to taunt her. She was sure now that Lyle had been having affairs all through their marriage. She'd been the stupid one then, but she wasn't going to be that way anymore.

Ryan was beginning to get restless and she knew he'd be hungry soon. She slipped around the edges of the room to the exit, where she saw McNally happily finalizing a sale with a buyer.

"Excuse me," she said.

McNally looked up, a polite smile in place. When he saw her, the smile turned into something genuine. "Hi. How's the little man holdin' up? This place is busier than a whore in—ah, sorry, ma'am. It's purty busy, though."

His embarrassment almost made her smile. "It's all right, McNally. I'm a rancher's daughter. I doubt you could say anything I haven't heard before." Then she indicated Ryan. "I'm going to take him back to the hotel. Would you let Tye know that we left?"

McNally's expression turned to one of mild distress. "Hey, now, don't you want to tell him yourself? I could easily—"

"No, I don't want to bother him." She was halfway out the door as she spoke. "Just tell him we'll be at the hotel."

* * *

Tye slipped his key card into the lock and opened the door of the suite. Ripping the string tie from his neck, he tossed it onto a nearby table, along with the jacket he shrugged off. If he'd ever hated an opening more, he couldn't remember when.

He wanted to be home. He could almost smell the leather of his saddle, could almost feel the rhythmic thud of his horse's hooves on the range. For years, he'd managed to tell himself he could live on the fringes of the West, photographing the lives of those who lived there, moving on to new vistas and new challenges. But he wasn't satisfied with that anymore. He'd forgotten, until the past year, how it felt to work the land every day, in every kind of weather there was.

He'd forgotten how much he needed to be close to the land.

Or maybe it wasn't that so much as that he'd realized he needed *land of his own.* Photographing other men working wasn't enough anymore. He'd spent a year now working someone else's spread, first his uncle's and then Dulcie's brother's land. And it just wasn't enough. He wanted—no, needed—to be checking his own fences, to be riding his own boundaries, to be responsible for his own herd.

And dammit, he wanted his own family to come home to at the end of the day. Where the hell had Dulcie disappeared to this evening? He strode into the bedroom, but the bedspread hadn't been turned back and she was nowhere in sight. He turned on his heel and crossed the suite to the other bedroom, hesitating long enough to allow his eyes to adjust to the dark before charging into the room.

Ryan was a small lump under the coverlet in the crib. He paused there for a moment, hunkering down to peer through the bars at his child. One little fist was jammed up against his mouth, as if he'd been trying to find his thumb, and his knees were drawn up under him, thrusting his diapered bottom into the air. Tye felt something inside him shift, as if his heart had grown a size and was pushing other organs out of the way. He pressed his forehead against the crib rail, fighting the sudden tightness that gripped his throat.

God, how he adored this little guy!

He'd all but forgiven Dulcie for not telling him about her pregnancy. After all, he wasn't going to miss much of Ryan's life. Besides, he had no one to blame but himself for not protecting her in the first place. He figured they could play the blame game for the rest of their lives, but the easiest thing to do was to let go of it and get on with making a family.

A small sound caught his attention and he stood, turning from the crib to survey the rest of the darkened room. Dulcie was sitting on the edge of the large bed, running her hands through her hair. "Tye?" she asked in a hushed voice. "What time is it?"

"Just after midnight," he told her.

She made no response, and after a moment, the pleasure he'd felt at coming home to her and his son began to fade again. He wondered if she resented him barging into the room unannounced, and his mood darkened further. He'd thought they were past that now.

"Are you coming to bed?" he asked.

Slowly, she turned her head in his direction. It was too dark for him to see her face, but there was no mistaking the distance in her tone when she said, "I'm sleeping in here tonight."

Well. That sounded final. He guessed there was nothing else to do but leave the room.

Afterward, he still wasn't sure why his body hadn't obeyed his conscious thoughts. All he knew was that rather than leaving the room as he'd intended, he'd stepped forward, using the hand she stretched out to ward him off to draw her closer, then clasping her around the waist and tossing her over his shoulder like a bag of oats.

She gave a muffled shriek against his back and he slapped her lightly on the rump. "Sh-h-h, you'll wake Ryan."

"I don't give a good—ouch!"

They were out of the bedroom, crossing the suite, and he'd slapped her again, a bit harder. "Now, now, Duls, ladies don't cuss."

"Then it's a damned good thing I'm not a lady. Put me down."

He did, dumping her into the middle of his king-size bed with a flourish.

She bounced once, scrambling off the side to glare at him with her hands on her hips. Through clenched teeth, she said, "I've never been a big fan of the cave-man routine."

"Me neither." He was starting to feel a whole lot better. He'd bet it would be a long time before she tried to freeze him out again.

"Did you drag me over here for a reason?"

"Yup."

He made a production out of emptying his pockets onto the dresser, then walked across the room to a chair and settled himself into it. When he met her gaze, her eyes were hot with resentment. For a second, he was taken aback but he only said, "I got worried when I couldn't find you tonight."

Their eyes locked. She was the one who looked away first. "I told McNally I was leaving."

"Why didn't you let me know you were ready to leave? I would have brought you home."

"You looked busy."

He regarded her thoughtfully. She still hadn't looked at him. Instead, she was running her finger industriously over the curve of the bedpost.

"What's going on here, Dulcie?" he asked her quietly. "I thought we were beginning to communicate pretty well. But tonight you ran out on me and now I feel like we're back to where we started when I found you again."

"I felt like I was invisible tonight," she said.

He was startled, and stung by the accusatory tone. "I introduced you to McNally," he said defensively. "You wouldn't come with me when I started to make my rounds, remember?"

"I remember." Her voice sounded weary. "I wasn't about to have perfect strangers asking if I was your wife and giving me sly looks when I said no."

"Someone did that?"

"No," she said. "But your friend McNally was the only one you introduced me to and he was too polite."

Tye threw his hands in the air. "Doggone it, Duls. I don't understand why you're mad. I've asked you to marry me. You're the one who doesn't want to be Mrs. Tye Bradshaw."

"And if this is what it would be like, I'm glad I haven't agreed!"

He slouched in the chair, unwilling to let her see how the words hurt. "I thought I was respecting your wishes when you said you didn't want to be introduced around."

She sighed and sat down on the edge of the bed as if she were a balloon that had lost too much air to stay aloft. In a small voice, she said, "I'm sorry, Tye. I'm being unreasonable. I'm the one who asked to be left alone. But once I was, I wasn't happy. Every time I looked around, there seemed to be another pretty woman hanging on you."

She didn't have to say the rest, that it must have brought back unhappy memories from her marriage. "I thought I was doing what you wanted," he said. "You seemed to want anonymity. I was trying to respect that."

He rose and walked across the room, sitting on the bed beside her. "Dulcie, I don't particularly enjoy those things. In the future, I'm going to be doing fewer of them." He picked up her hand and threaded his fingers through her much smaller ones, drawing her to her feet before him. In bare feet, she was even smaller than usual, and all his protective instincts were aroused. "I'm not your ex-husband. I'm not going to cheat on you." He almost smiled, placing his hands at her shoulders and massaging gently. "Hell, you're too much of a handful for me to be thinking about adding any more."

She sniffed. "You make me sound like a horse."

He laughed, drawing her closer. "There's no way I could ever mistake you for a filly." The press of her breasts against him was a sweet pleasure, distracting him from the serious discussion he knew they needed to have. Dropping his head, he sought her mouth as he slid his arms more fully around her.

She moaned softly at the fit of their bodies; he swallowed the sound and elicited more. Backing her toward the bed, he swiftly removed her outer garments while she unbuttoned his shirt and opened his pants. When her hands dipped inside, it was his turn to moan.

"I shouldn't touch you until we're done talking," he panted, following her down and covering her soft, curving form with his. "Every time I do, you make me forget what I wanted to say."

She smiled against his lips. "I'm the one who gets distracted. You—" She dragged in a gasp of surprise when he moved her legs apart and entered her without waiting. He groaned at the tight clasp of her body, then groaned again when, instead of tensing, she relaxed her legs and grasped his buttocks, urging him deeper into her welcoming depths, arching against him again and again until his body couldn't withstand her feminine invitation any longer. As he doubled his rhythm and release swept over him, he dimly realized she was with him, gently clutching his buried length in repeated pulses of her own ecstasy, pushing him beyond satiation to a new realm of shared intimacy that cemented his need for her in a way that even the child they shared had never done.

The following afternoon, she was unpacking her things in her room at the ranch when Angel came breezing in.

"Welcome home! How was your trip?"

Dulcie considered the question as she hugged her sister-in-law. "The trip was . . . good for me."

Angel looked surprised. "That's what Day said, but I didn't think you'd admit it."

Dulcie grimaced. "God, I hate being so predictable."

"You're not." Angel smiled. "Day figured you'd die before you would admit that you needed to get away from the ranch for even a minute." Then her pretty face sobered, revealing her concern. "So it went well?"

Dulcie shrugged. "I suppose so. Traveling with Ryan went much better than I thought it would. He slept the whole way there and the whole way back."

"And Tye's opening?"

"Ryan was fine. I was pretty uptight." She unzipped her cosmetics bag and began returning items to their accustomed places, then looked squarely at Angel. "Honestly?"

When the taller woman nodded, she went on. "Sometimes I look at Tye and I don't see him. In my mind, I'm still expecting him to behave like Lyle did. Lyle would have flirted outrageously with every woman at the show. Tye was nothing like that, but I'm so afraid to trust my own judgment that I lower my horns and charge sometimes before he even knows what's wrong."

Angel looked sympathetic but her smile held secret laughter. "Don't be too hard on yourself. Tye seems to me to be pretty adept at getting out of the way and distracting you before you can wound him."

"He is." Now it was Dulcie's turn to smile reluctantly. "It's a little scary to have someone be able to read me so well."

"Yes, but it can be pretty wonderful, too," Angel said. "Did you ever feel that way with Lyle?"

"Never." On that point she was positive. "The very first time Tye and I ever went out to dinner, I came home wishing my husband was as easy to talk to. And that was when I thought we were only friends."

"Soooo..." Angel drew out the word. "Does this mean you're going to marry the poor guy and put him out of his misery?"

Dulcie's feeling of contentment fled. Quietly, she said, "No. No, I'm not."

"But why?" Angel's expression was a study in bewilderment. "You love him, don't you?"

"Yes, I love him." It was almost as hard to say the words aloud to herself as it was to say them to Angel. "But I don't want to be the one who gets left behind in a marriage ever again. Tye might want me now, but that won't last. His job requires lots of travel. I won't travel for the rest of my life and I won't live with a man whose fidelity is tested on every trip."

Angel was frowning. Dulcie dreaded her next words. Angel was so sweet and pliant that she hardly ever dug in her heels, but when she did . . . it was best to be in the next county.

"If you had been married to a nine-to-five guy the first time around, do you think you would still be married?" Angel's face was a study in concentration. She awaited the answer like a hawk watching for its next meal to emerge.

Dulcie hesitated. But honesty forced her to examine the question. "Well, no. I don't think it would have made much difference. Looking back, I just don't think Lyle was the faithful kind."

"So fidelity has nothing to do with proximity?"

"I didn't say that."

"Oh, yes you did." Angel shook her finger under Dulcie's nose. "You know what? I don't think this is really about whether or not you think Tye will cheat on you. I think that deep in your heart you know exactly what kind of man he is and that you needn't judge him by anyone else's actions. But you're scared. You'd rather not take a chance on letting somebody get too close to you. Maybe that's why you married someone you weren't particularly close to the first time around.''

"Pop psychology." Dulcie waved her hand dismissively, but the words lodged in her heart. Was Angel right? And if she was, didn't that make her a pretty shallow person? Aloud, she said, "I sense our first serious disagreement since we've been sisters coming on. Let's change the subject."

Angel regarded her for a long moment, then stepped forward and drew her into a warm embrace. "I'm sorry if I was out of line, Duls. I just want to see you happy."

As Tye came down the hallway with his duffel bag, his booted feet rang out on the polished floorboards before he reached the rug runner that covered much of the floor. He was about to pass the closed door of Dulcie's room, but it opened and Angel's blond mane emerged.

"Hi, Tye. Welcome home. Things have been pretty quiet around here without the three of you."

"I bet it was a welcome change," he said dryly.

She made a face. "Too quiet." Then she turned, and he saw Dulcie in the room behind her. "But all that will change in a few months."

Dulcie's gaze had locked with his, but at Angel's words she turned to her sister-in-law. "What are you talking about?"

Angel paused, holding out a hand to each of them. As her face lit with happiness, Tye knew what her next words were going to be.

"I'm expecting a baby!"

"You're—Angel!" Dulcie shrieked and launched herself at her friend. "Why didn't you tell me right away?"

Angel shrugged, accepting Dulcie's hugs and Tye's handclasp. "We had other things to discuss. Besides, I wanted to tell you both together that Ryan will be getting a cousin."

"This is great news," he said with feeling.

"Oh…" Dulcie's eyes were shiny and wet. "This is wonderful. Congratulations! Let's see, October, November—will this be a Christmas baby?" At Angel's nod, she wriggled all over, like an ecstatic puppy.

Only thing was, he thought, the effect her jiggling and wiggling had on him was definitely not the effect of a puppy.

"That's a great time of year," Dulcie was saying. "Things are pretty slow for two or three months there. You'll have plenty of time to devote to the baby before calving starts. How perfect!"

As the two women enthused, Tye gave Angel a warm hug and then started on down the hallway to deposit his bag in the room he'd come to regard as his. But his mood was dark.

They were back on the ranch, back where Dulcie belonged. He could see it so clearly now, with something as simple as her comment to Angel. For Dulcie, life revolved around the Red Arrow. Everything she did she equated with how it would fit into the work schedule on the ranch.

He'd thought that if he owned another ranch, she could simply transfer her energies there, but now he wasn't so sure. It wasn't a matter of energy. It was a matter of happiness. This was where she belonged. Not some other spread, some other place. She'd been born here, had lived most of her life on this soil, and was perfectly happy at the notion that she'd do the same with Ryan.

He, Tye, was the only superfluous piece of information in the whole equation.

Ryan had changed so much from the helpless little bundle she'd held in her arms on his first day of life. Dulcie sat in her favorite chair in the living room, holding him propped in her lap. They had just finished the evening feeding, and as she patted, the baby gave a huge bubble. Pleased, she cradled him in her arms and looked down into his wide eyes.

"What a wonderful little man you are. You're going to grow up to be the biggest, fastest roper—"

A wide grin stretched Ryan's mobile mouth. For weeks, he'd yawned, grimaced, screwed up his face in displeasure, but this! This was a real smile. He wasn't gazing into space, he was looking at *her*, his mother.

Automatically, she raised her head, seeking Tye. Instantly she realized that he had yet to join them in the family room. She glanced at the clock, slightly disturbed. Tye rarely missed an evening feeding for anything other than work that couldn't wait. He hadn't mentioned anything to her this evening about going out to the barn, which was his custom if he was needed.

She rose to her feet, still smiling down at Ryan. Tye had to see this!

Five minutes later, she was knocking on the closed door of his bedroom. She'd looked everywhere else in the house, and Day had told her he wasn't in the barn, so she'd come here as a last resort.

"Tye?"

The door opened. He stood framed in the doorway, his expression questioning. "What's wrong?"

"Nothing's wrong." She smiled and indicated their son. "After I fed him, I was holding him and talking to him, and he smiled at me. A real smile, not one of those 'gas grins' you laugh about."

Tye's eyes widened and he held out his arms for the baby. "You're kidding! I can't believe I missed it." He settled Ryan into the curve of his arm and peered into the child's face. "Hey, buddy, are you going to smile at me, too? Or is that reserved just for your mother? I know she's pretty special, so I can't really blame you for that." After a moment, when Ryan's eyes rounded and he looked blankly up at his father, Tye laughed. "Oh, well, I guess one a day is all he's prepared to offer."

Then he took Dulcie's elbow, steering her into the room. "I need to talk to you. Come in here a minute."

She allowed him to lead her into the room, but when she saw the open duffel bag on the bed, she couldn't hold back a small intake of dismayed breath. "Why are you packing?"

He still held her arm, his long fingers gently rubbing back and forth over the soft skin inside her biceps. "I talked to McNally tonight. He has an important job for me. I'll be on assignment for about a week."

"Will you...are you planning on returning to the ranch when you're finished?" She couldn't look at him, couldn't let him see the devastation she felt at the words.

He hesitated, and her heartbeat stalled in disappointment, as heavy as a stone placed in her chest. Then he said, "I'd like that, if you want me to," and she could breathe again.

"Of course we want you to," she said, aware that her voice was too hearty but unable to allow herself any softer tone for fear she would cry. "Ryan will miss his daddy." Then, before he could respond, she reached over and took the baby from his arms, beating a hasty retreat. "I have to get him to bed now."

She made it into Ryan's room before the tears began to fall. By the time she had laid him down and gently covered him, she could barely see.

The hand that touched her shoulder made her jump. "Duls."

Quickly she turned her back to Tye, unwilling to let him see her tears. But she couldn't control the ragged sob that burst from her as he came around in front of her. Then he placed his arms around her and drew her against his chest, rocking her slightly from side to side as her hot tears soaked his shirt.

"Will you miss me, too?"

"You know I will." She couldn't seem to halt the tears. The sweet comfort he offered only made her all the more aware that he was leaving.

"I promise I'll be back." He reached around her to pull a tissue from Ryan's dresser, then mopped her face before handing it to her.

She blew her nose loudly. "I'm sorry. I guess those good ol' pregnancy hormones haven't gone away yet."

"Don't hide your feelings from me. Please." He took her hand, turned it up and pressed a gentle kiss into her palm. "Will you sleep with me tonight?"

"Yes."

He led her down the hall from Ryan's room to his own, stepping back to allow her to precede him. He didn't turn on the light but closed the door and locked it after retrieving the baby monitor from her room and placing it on the table by the door.

Then he straightened, gathering her into his arms as if she were the most precious treasure imaginable, fragile and easily damaged. His flesh was warm everywhere he touched her, his hands tender. He cupped her jaw, tilting her face up for his kiss. His hand slid into her hair, spearing through the thick, silky strands to cradle her skull.

It was a curiously intimate feeling, standing there before him, caught by the lightest pressure of his hand on her head. The tips of her breasts brushed his chest, his thighs pressed ever so lightly against her. She had always associated their lovemaking with fierce emotion, with the surging force of desire that carried them along in its wake, but tonight was different.

He'd shown her tenderness before. But tonight...tonight *was* tenderness. Tonight was his mouth, soft and slick, moving against and inside hers so sweetly that she felt the tears awake to slide down her cheeks again even as she kissed him back. Tonight was fumbling fingers carefully brushing aside layers of clothing. Tonight was bodies touching as if for the first time, gasps of delight at the perfect fit of masculine demand against feminine surrender, sighs of wonder at the radiating pleasure exploring hands and mouths brought to intimate places previously uninitiated.

He trailed his mouth down the sensitive column of her neck and over the crest of a swollen nipple, dropping to his knees before her, and she took heady pleasure in the sight of her own breasts covered by his large palms, her belly, her thighs, at which he worshiped. Her knees grew weak when his tongue found her, and she widened her stance in deliberate invitation, offering him access to the moist treasure he sought.

With an incoherent sound of male satisfaction, Tye pressed her backward, pushing her into a sitting position on the edge of his bed. He continued to kneel between her spread thighs, drinking deeply of the sweetness she offered him. She braced herself with her hands behind her; her head fell backward. Her belly gathered itself into a taut knot of quivering excite-

ment; release hovered just beyond her reach as her
hips rose and fell in rhythm with the demands of his
mouth.

"Let go," he breathed against her. "Let it go,
baby."

"I can't." She was sobbing, clutching at him with
frantic hands, begging him to end the torment.
"Please, please." Her head thrashed from side to side
as he surged up onto her, into her in one mighty motion that joined them fully. Then, driven beyond his
own control by her writhing, heaving body beneath
him, he established a hard, driving rhythm that
quickly brought her to the release she'd awaited. As
her body convulsed, gripping him in ecstatic pulses of
completion, he thrust madly a final time, making her
cry out and clutch him more tightly as he poured
himself into her warm body.

Nine

Tye brought Ryan to her just before dawn, holding both of them in a close embrace while Dulcie nursed their son. Then, as she slipped back into slumber, he kissed her once, murmured, "I'll be back in a week," and left.

When she awoke the next time, she was snuggled deep into Tye's bed with Ryan at her side, wailing lustily. A glance at the clock as she took him to his own room for a diaper change before feeding him told her it was nearly eight.

Going down to breakfast, she couldn't prevent the spring in her step, the smile that kept assigning itself to her lips. She felt as bouncy and full of optimism as a helium balloon, able to consider plans and decisions that only days before had overwhelmed her.

Tye might not love her, but he surely desired her. They had a lot in common, and he'd told her himself that he wanted to travel less. They shared a son.

And she loved him.

Bottom line, that was what mattered. Going to Santa Fe with him had opened her eyes to the differences in their lives, but strangely enough, after all the hours she'd spent dreading it, the trip hadn't been so bad. And it would have been even better if she hadn't allowed her insecurities to come between them.

She loved Tye. She could adjust to his traveling; she could even choose to go with him on occasion. She wasn't tied to the ranch anymore by her fears; she was there because she wanted to be, because this was the life she loved.

When Tye returned...the next time he asked her to marry him, she was going to accept. They could live at the Red Arrow when he wasn't on assignment; their children could be raised to learn ranch operation alongside their cousins as she and Day had been raised.

She'd learned the hard way that life didn't turn out to be the rosy future all children envisioned. She was going to take what she could get and not whine if she didn't have it all.

Damn the weather, anyway! Tye looked out the window of his room at the overcast skies the following Friday. He had taken this assignment covering the opening of a new hunting lodge in Oregon because the amount and variety of wildlife in the area offered a challenge, and he thought that if anything could shake him out of this insane desire to be a rancher, something new and untried might do the trick.

Instead, he could say with certainty that all he wanted to do was get back to New Mexico and some land of his own, land where he and Dulcie could work and raise Ryan together.

But he wasn't one to abandon something he'd started. He'd finish this photo assignment before he started pursuing the rest of his life, if he had to wait out a week of rain.

Looking out the window, he was afraid that was exactly what might happen. Although he could do a certain amount of work regardless of the weather, for a well-balanced shoot there were a few critical shots he had in mind that absolutely required at least a few rays of sunshine.

He glanced at his watch, then reached for the phone. Though he'd rarely had the need to use them, he had the numbers for the Red Arrow memorized.

A moment later, the ringing stopped abruptly as someone lifted the receiver at the ranch. "Red Arrow."

"Hello, Red Arrow." He was absurdly pleased that Dulcie had answered.

"Tye!" Her voice lilted in clear delight, then lowered to a throaty purr. "I've missed you."

"I've missed you, too." He shifted position, amazed that just the sound of her voice could affect his body so strongly. "And Ryan. How's my little cowboy?"

"Smiling all the time. Just wait till he sees you. You won't believe it."

"I miss holding him. And you." He cleared his throat. "Hard to believe that two months ago I didn't know he existed, and I hadn't seen you in almost a year." He sighed into the phone. "It's pretty pathetic when a grown man has to admit he's so lonely he just wants to come home."

She chuckled. "Not so pathetic. We want you home as much as you want to be here. So when are you coming?"

Some of the happiness he'd felt at the sound of her voice melted away. "I don't know yet. I'd thought I'd be leaving tomorrow, but the weather isn't cooperating. I have to stay until I get a little sunshine, maybe three or four days."

She didn't say anything for a moment and he could almost feel her withdrawing.

"Duls?"

"I'm still here." Her voice had lost its bounce. "I'm sorry you'll be delayed. But I know this is your job. Take as much time as you like."

But I don't want to take any more time, he wanted to shout. *I want to come home!* But he didn't say it. He would have to wait until he had her in his arms again to reassure her that she was all he'd been thinking about.

They exchanged small talk about the ranch, about the weather. She told him he didn't have to call her every time his assignment stretched out longer than expected. When he finally hung up, he was ready to punch something with his bare fists.

What lousy timing! After all he knew about her first marriage, he knew she had to be feeling insecure about his absence. He flopped down on his bed and stared angrily at the ceiling. Maybe he was crazy to think he could make her happy. Maybe she was right to refuse his offer of marriage. Maybe they were just too different to ever be able to make their relationship work.

But where did that leave Ryan? Although Dulcie's unquestioning acceptance of him as the father of her son had gone a long way toward easing the sting of his past, he still worried for Ryan's sake. Illegitimacy didn't have to ruin your life if you were surrounded by a close, loving family as he had been. He'd had to become an adult who was accepted for who he was rather than what he was, before he had realized just how little the circumstances of his birth could affect his life.

But still... maybe he could offer Dulcie some sort of deal. What that might be, he couldn't imagine right now. But perhaps she would consider marrying him in name only and letting him adopt Ryan formally—

This was all so crazy!

And it all came back to Dulcie, no matter which way he twisted his thoughts. If only he didn't miss her, and need her, so much.

He pushed himself off the bed and grabbed his cameras. If he couldn't complete his assignment, he'd go looking for something—anything!—else to shoot. Anything was better than lying here missing Dulcie so badly that he was ready to throw in the towel in the middle of a job and go crawling home.

Two days later, he'd decided the sun was never going to shine on the Northwest again. And he didn't care. He'd wrapped up the shoot, using different filters to achieve something of the look he'd initially envisioned. If they didn't work out, too bad. What he had finished already would be adequate, if not outstanding.

The telephone rang as he was stuffing clothes into his duffel bag. Snatching it up, he almost expected, for a single, hope-filled moment, to hear Dulcie's voice on the other end. But it was his lawyer. Negotiations on the Moser ranch had been completed. It was his if he wanted it. *If he wanted it!*

Six hours later, he was nearly home, having picked up his car from the airport where he'd left it parked and driven straight to Deming, where he'd met his lawyer at the local real estate office. He'd handed over a check for a ridiculous amount of money, but still he found himself euphoric. He was a landowner. The ranch next to the Red Arrow belonged to him.

And Dulcie, if she would have him. They could work the ranch together. They could raise Ryan with two parents and a family name, and maybe even give him a few brothers and sisters. He grinned, pleased with the novel thought. Who'd ever have thought Tye Bradshaw would be dreaming about babies?

His travel camera banged against his chest as he parked his car in the ranch yard and strode toward the house, and he glanced down at it reflectively. He didn't doubt that it would always be a part of his life, but he knew now that he would never go back to roving the country in search of the perfect photograph. The fervor he'd once felt, the quest for perfection, was gone.

It had been replaced by a deep determination to wrest a living from the inhospitable land of the Southwest. The land was calling.

He entered the house through the back door that everyone used. Angel was in the kitchen; Beth Ann was "painting" with pudding industriously on a large sheet of freezer paper while Ryan surveyed the world from his little seat atop the table.

He dropped his bag near the door to the hall, removing his camera from around his neck and setting it atop the refrigerator where little fingers couldn't investigate. His other cameras were still in the car; he'd have to bring them in soon or risk heat damage, but right now he couldn't wait to greet his family.

"Hi, squirt! You been taking care of your cousin?" He scooped Beth Ann out of her chair, avoiding small, messy fingers and nuzzling her neck.

"Uh-huh." She planted a loud, wet kiss on his cheek. "I think he said my name this morning."

Tye grinned. "Wow. That would really be something." Over her head he smiled at Angel, who rolled her eyes.

"Welcome home, Tye," she said.

"Thanks," he replied seriously. "You don't know how good it is to be home."

"Oh, yes I do." She nodded knowingly. "I wasn't raised here, don't forget. I doubt I'll ever take it for granted the way they do." Then she smiled and jerked her head in the direction of the ceiling. "Dulcie's upstairs changing beds."

"Let me say hello to my boy here before I go find his mother." He carefully lifted Ryan out of the infant seat, talking baby talk to him. Ryan's little mouth moved, and his whole body increased its frenetic activity as he recognized the person holding him. Finally, his lips spread wide, tilting up in a clearly recognizable smile while drool moistened his chin.

Tye thought his heart would crack in two. He snuggled the baby for a moment longer, but he couldn't wait to talk to Dulcie. With a murmured apology to his son, he laid him back in his seat, snagged his gear and headed up the stairs.

A pile of sheets in the hallway indicated that she was, indeed, changing beds. As he paused to listen for her, a pile of bedding flew out of Beth Ann's doorway and landed in a lump in the hall. Dulcie followed it at a slower pace, dusting her hands together.

She stopped when she saw him and her face lit up like a lamp just switched on. "Tye!"

He strode toward her, intending to take her in his arms, needing to kiss her senseless more than he'd ever needed anything in his life, but before he could reach her, she schooled her face into a more guarded expression and bent to gather the sheets into her arms. When he reached her side, he stopped, frustrated and unsure, without embracing her. She stood facing him, hugging the sheets to her in a movement that almost, if he were the imaginative type, appeared defensive.

What the hell was going on here? "I'm home," he said unnecessarily.

She smiled, and the little dimple in her left cheek he so liked to kiss appeared to taunt him. "Welcome home. Ryan's downstairs."

"I saw him." Memory warmed his voice. "He smiled at me."

"I told you it wouldn't be long before he'd be doing it regularly," she reminded him.

He nodded, searching her face for a hint of her feelings, but her gaze was shuttered, with only an impersonal friendliness on display. "I'm going to be moving soon," he said abruptly, hoping to provoke a reaction from her.

For the barest instant, he thought he'd succeeded. Shock bloomed in her eyes. It was followed for a moment by another emotion—sadness, he thought—but he couldn't be sure because she quickly masked it, nodding vigorously.

"Thank you for spending this time with Ryan," she said. "I hope you know you'll always be welcome here. We'd like to know how you're doing and I'd like Ryan to be able to get to know you."

Baldly, he asked, "Doesn't it bother you that I'm leaving?"

She hesitated, and he wondered if his question had shaken her out of that damned reserve she'd donned. Then she nodded. "Yes, it makes me sad. Ryan will miss seeing you every day." She took a deep breath. "But I also have to thank you, Tye. You've helped me to see that the Red Arrow isn't a place to escape from the world. I could go anywhere if I had to.''

"You'd leave the ranch?''

''I didn't say that,'' she corrected. ''I'm staying here, but not because I have to. This is a conscious choice, a life I want our son to grow into as he grows up. We'll always be right here, and you have a standing invitation to visit anytime.''

He felt bewildered. Anger was roiling in his gut, too. All he'd wanted was to get home to her, to share his big news about the other ranch with her, to hold her and touch her and quench the powerful thirst he'd developed for her.

And she was brushing him off.

He couldn't address it rationally, couldn't think straight enough to frame a question, to press her, to maybe crack that damned wall of reserve with logic. Waves of hurt were rolling over him; he encouraged the accompanying anger and squelched the pain. How, after all they had shared, could she treat him so casually?

He wasn't just a friend. He wasn't just the father of her son. He wasn't just some convenient, out-of-sight, out-of-mind date with whom she shared occasional, casual sex.

He was her lover. But more important, *he was the man who loved her.*

The thought struck him with no warning. But it didn't amaze him, didn't stagger him in any way. He supposed he'd known it since the day she'd come apart in his arms in that Albuquerque apartment. When he'd entered her body that first, shattering night, she'd entered his heart, as well.

She'd been there while he'd worked in Montana and since he'd come back to New Mexico after her, she'd taken over more and more of it every day. He wanted to savor the feeling, but he couldn't.

Right now he was so damned mad at her he could wring her neck.

He stared at her with hot, angry eyes, as she stood there before him and tried to pretend they were having a nice, civilized conversation about child-rearing and visitation. Once again she was hiding something from him, something he knew was within her, something he was determined to unleash.

In a voice silky with menace, he said, "So I'm welcome to visit anytime?"

It went right over her head, probably because she was trying so hard to convince him he didn't matter. "Anytime," she confirmed blithely.

His hands shot out so fast that she never saw them coming, fastening around her waist and dragging her against him, disregarding the sheets she dropped to the floor. "How 'bout between dusk and dawn every night?"

She began to struggle immediately, looking down at his imprisoning hands rather than into his eyes as she said, "That wasn't what I meant. I thought we were discussing Ryan."

"And I thought we were discussing *us*." He caught her jaw between two inflexible fingers and forced her to look at him. "I had the impression you wanted me

in your life. I left you warming my bed when I went
off on this last assignment, and now you're telling me
the most I can hope for is occasional visits with my
son? Is this a polite way of telling me you don't want
me anymore?''

Her lower lip quivered and she shielded her gaze
with her long lashes; he was holding her face immobile but he couldn't force her to look at him.

"I've told you from the beginning that I couldn't
marry you—"

"I didn't mention marriage just now!" he roared,
ignoring the way she flinched. "I want to know—oh,
the hell with it."

He took her mouth roughly, abruptly, sure that
there was at least one way she did still want him and
determined to find out. But when his anger met that
quivering bottom lip, it evaporated under a rush of
tenderness he hadn't been expecting. His hands, rigid
with his rage, gentled, molding her against his body
from breast to thigh with sweet persuasion as his
mouth molded hers, giving her all the unspoken passion he'd wanted to share with her for days.

At first she was reserved, still beneath his on-
slaught. Then, as his tongue demanded and won en-
try into the sweet inner recesses of her mouth, she
appeared to rouse from whatever stasis had held her
immobile, and she returned his caresses with a fiery
passion, tilting her mouth up and pressing her body
into his in a manner that left him in no doubt of his
welcome. He showed her without words what she

meant to him, drinking her response from her lips and begging for more.

He wanted to make love to her, to claim her body completely so she couldn't forget again that she was his, and he knew by the way she clung to him and offered herself for his caresses that that was what she wanted, too.

But finally his mind began to protest.

They'd known each other intimately, they shared a child, but they needed to talk. As badly as he wanted her, he knew desire wasn't enough. Not this time.

Gradually, he ended their mouth play, weaning her from him until he was holding her loosely while she stood dazed in his arms. She stared blankly at nothing when he gently said, "Dulcie?"

When her gaze shifted to him, he was startled by the hopeless look in the depths of her dark eyes, but he went on. "What happened while I was gone? To change your feelings, I mean. I know that when I left here you were happy." He pressed a gentle kiss against her forehead and felt her indrawn breath, almost like a sob. "You cared for me then, and I think you still do. I know that physically we're a great match. But that's not all I want from you. We have to be able to talk to each other."

Except for her warm flesh and shallow breaths, she could have been a statue in his arms. Finally, she drew in a deep breath and began to speak. "I thought I could do it, marry you and take what you offered. I thought th   Ryan and I lived here, I wouldn't mind your constant traveling. When you left   told myself that the next time you asked me to marry you, I'd say yes. I was determined to give it a try. And then..." Her voice trailed away.

He forced himself to be patient, to wait while she sorted through her thoughts and explained. "And then . . . ?"

"And then you called and said you'd be delayed." She shook her head, her eyes filling with tears. "Tye, I was counting the hours until you came home. When you called and couldn't make it, it was like somebody put a stick of dynamite in my mind. The reminders of every phone call Lyle had ever made, every lie he ever told me, floated to the surface." She held up a hand when he would have spoken. "I know you aren't Lyle. But I also wonder when, or if, I'll ever be free of the doubts he instilled in me. When we were first married, he used to call at the last minute and tell me he'd be a few days more. Gradually, he stopped calling altogether and stayed away more and more."

"But you've said yourself I'm not Lyle," he protested, hearing the desperation in his voice but beyond caring. He felt as if he were swiping at invisible cobwebs—no matter how many he cut down, there might always be one more lurking somewhere, waiting to ambush his happiness.

"I know you aren't." She put a tender hand to the side of his face, closing her eyes when he turned his head and kissed the palm. "Tye, I love you. I love you far too much. I lost one man like that but I couldn't survive it if I lost you. I just don't want to take that kind of risk with my heart."

"This isn't an issue of love," he said sadly, fighting to keep the bitterness from his voice. He'd only realized recently how badly he needed to hear those words, but she was taking all the joy out of the declaration. How could she love him and not want to be with him for the rest of their lives? "This is an issue of trust. I understand it's a huge leap, given what you've already lived through."

"This has everything to do with love." The corners of her mouth lifted in a small smile that tore another hole in his aching heart. "I could never have cared for Lyle the way I care for you. But I settled for half a marriage once and I just can't do it again." She stared at him, the strong spirit that had drawn him to her shining from her eyes. "Think about me, about how I feel left behind while you're off globe-trotting." Her voice gentled and her tone rang with finality. "You would break my heart."

"How do you know that? You said yourself that I'm not your first husband. Dulcie, there have been no other women in my life since I met you. There never will be. Why don't you stop trying to protect yourself from heartbreak and give happiness a try?"

She hesitated, then, without saying a word, he could see that she was going to refuse.

"How can you make a decision that will affect you, me and our son without at least hearing the plans I've made for our future?"

She shook her head, afraid to hope. That was the bad thing about loving Tye—he made her want to believe anything was possible. *But it isn't,* she reminded herself. *You'll only get your heart broken if you let him talk you into something you'll regret.*

But Tye wasn't listening to her silent argument with herself. He caught her hands and brought them up between them. "You said you loved me, but you didn't give me a chance to enjoy it. Listen now, and no matter what happens, savor this, I love you, too. I was attracted to you from the first day we met. The first time we made love, my life changed forever. You haven't been far from my heart since. Why else would I chase you from Montana clear to New Mexico? And don't forget, that was before I knew we had made a child together." He smiled at the thought of their son, grinning his lopsided little grin. "Loving you, sharing Ryan with you, has been the best thing that's ever happened to me. It's changed my life in so many ways, and all of them are good."

He took a deep breath and looked deep into her eyes. "Dulcie, the place I'm moving...I bought the Moser ranch. If you'll marry me, we'll be living there, within spitting distance of your family. We can start our own herd, raise Ryan in a home of his own."

Then he remembered the best part, the most important part. "I won't be away much at all, but when I do have to travel, my family can come with me. I don't know, maybe I'm having my midlife crisis early, but I'm planning a major career change—from photography to livestock. I'd like to set up a cow-calf operation," he said, trying to gauge her reaction.

There was none. She simply looked at him blankly. Then she opened her mouth, hesitated and shook her head, before closing it again without saying a word.

His heart grew leaden as he interpreted her actions. She was going to refuse him.

All the old feelings of not being good enough flooded back. He'd spent his formative years feeling as if he was always on the outside looking in, and now he was going to spend the rest of his feeling the same way. Oh, he'd made peace with his past. He knew that his family loved him, that his friends measured him by the man he'd become rather than the circumstances of his birth. But all that was unimportant beside the fact that he was going to be alone for the rest of his life, longing for the one thing he could never have.

Slowly, his arms dropped away from her. He turned toward the stairs, seeing years of loneliness and regret stretch before him, years of greeting the woman he loved casually at the door while he waited for short visits with the son they shared.

He might as well go get the keys to his own place and start making a list of what needed to be done. It wouldn't be the same without Dulcie, but for Ryan's sake, he'd have to try to make it home—

"Tye?"

If he'd been thinking any louder, he wouldn't have heard her. Slowly, he looked over his shoulder at her. He wondered if she knew how tough this was for him, if discussions about child custody and all that could wait until later, until he'd had a chance to get past the prospect of the bleak, lonely future that stared him down.

When his gaze met hers, he got a jolt.

She was smiling. Not a lot, but a small, tentative smile. "Could you use a small herd of branded cattle to get started?"

He could only stare at her, wondering what she meant . . . and afraid to speculate on what he thought it might mean, in case he was wrong. Finally, he shook his head. "I couldn't accept that."

Her smile widened. "It's going to look odd if I leave my cattle behind when I move to the new place."

His depression lifted as her words penetrated. Still, he was afraid to hope. "Since when were you planning on moving?"

She came toward him, lifting her hands to clasp the ones he extended. "Since a few seconds ago when I realized I'd spend the rest of my life regretting it if I let you walk out of here without me." She raised their clasped hands and kissed his knuckles. "I'm sorry for letting my doubts get in the way of the best thing that's ever happened in my life. If you'll still have me, I'd like to marry you."

He couldn't prevent the giddy smile that split his face, but his voice was serious and deep. "I'll have you."

She chuckled, sensual awareness flaring in her eyes. "Is that a promise?"

He nodded, his expression growing even more intense. "It is. I'll have you in every way there is. In rich times and poor ones, in sickness, in health, in body, in spirit and most definitely in love for the rest of our lives together. Does that cover it?''

She nodded her head as she reached, on tiptoe to fling her arms around him and press her lips to his. "That covers it, cowboy. I love you."

"And I love you, cowgirl." He lifted her off the floor and whirled her in a dizzy circle down the hall and into her bedroom before setting her on her feet and turning to lock the door. "Do you think anybody will mind if we take a quick siesta?"

* * * * *

The collection of the year!
NEW YORK TIMES BESTSELLING AUTHORS

Linda Lael Miller
Wild About Harry

Janet Dailey
Sweet Promise

Elizabeth Lowell
Reckless Love

Penny Jordan
Love's Choices

and featuring
Nora Roberts
The Calhoun Women

This special trade-size edition features four of the wildly
popular titles in the Calhoun miniseries together in
one volume—a true collector's item!

Pick up these great authors and a chance to win
a weekend for two in New York City at the
Marriott Marquis Hotel on Broadway! We'll pay
for your flight, your hotel—even a Broadway show!

Available in December at your favorite retail outlet.

NEW YORK
Marriott.
MARQUIS

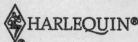 

NYT1296-R

Take 4 bestselling love stories FREE

Plus get a FREE surprise gift!

As seen on TV!
Free Gift Offer

With a Free Gift proof-of-purchase from any Silhouette® book,
you can receive a beautiful cubic zirconia pendant.

This gorgeous marquise-shaped stone is a genuine cubic
zirconia—accented by an 18" gold tone necklace.

(Approximate retail value $19.95)

Send for yours today...
compliments of ▼ *Silhouette*®
TM

To receive your free gift, a cubic zirconia pendant, send us one original proof-of-
purchase, photocopies not accepted, from the back of any Silhouette Romance™,
Silhouette Desire®, Silhouette Special Edition®, Silhouette Intimate Moments®
or Silhouette Yours Truly™ title available in August, September or October at your favorite
retail outlet, together with the Free Gift Certificate, plus a check or money order for
$1.65 U.S./$2.15 CAN. (do not send cash) to cover postage and handling, payable
to Silhouette Free Gift Offer. We will send you the specified gift. Allow 6 to 8 weeks for
delivery. Offer good until October 31, 1996 or while quantities last. Offer valid in the
U.S. and Canada only.

Free Gift Certificate

Name: _____

Address: _____

City: _____ State/Province: _____ Zip/Postal Code: _____

Mail this certificate, one proof-of-purchase and a check or money order for postage
and handling to: SILHOUETTE FREE GIFT OFFER 1996. In the U.S.: 3010 Walden
Avenue, P.O. Box 9077, Buffalo NY 14269-9077. In Canada: P.O. Box 613, Fort Erie,
Ontario L2Z 5X3.

FREE GIFT OFFER   084-KMD

ONE PROOF-OF-PURCHASE

To collect your fabulous FREE GIFT, a cubic zirconia pendant, you must include this
original proof-of-purchase for each gift with the properly completed Free Gift Certificate.

084-KMD

 HARLEQUIN® and  Silhouette®

are proud to present...

HERE COME THE GROOMS™

Four marriage-minded stories written by top
Harlequin and Silhouette authors!

Next month, you'll find:

The Bridal Price	by Barbara Boswell
Annie in the Morning	by Curtiss Ann Matlock
September Morning	by Diana Palmer
Outback Nights	by Emilie Richards

ADDED BONUS! In every edition of
Here Come the Grooms you'll find $5.00 worth
of coupons good for Harlequin and Silhouette
products.

On sale at your favorite Harlequin and Silhouette
retail outlet.

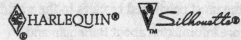 HARLEQUIN®  Silhouette®

Look us up on-line at: http://www.romance.net

You're About to Become a *Privileged Woman*

Reap the rewards of fabulous free gifts and benefits with proofs-of-purchase from Silhouette and Harlequin books

Pages & Privileges™

It's our way of thanking you for buying our books at your favorite retail stores.

**Harlequin and Silhouette—
the most privileged readers in the world!**

For more information about Harlequin and Silhouette's PAGES & PRIVILEGES program call the Pages & Privileges Benefits Desk: 1-503-794-2499